THE OVERTON ADVENTURES

THE
MUSELINGS

ED WICKE

INTERVARSITY PRESS
DOWNERS GROVE, ILLINOIS 60515

To the real Rachel, Robert and Alice

© *1990 by Ed Wicke*

Published in the United States of America by InterVarsity Press, Downers Grove, Illinois, with permission from Kingsway Publications Ltd., Eastbourne, E. Sussex, England.

InterVarsity Press is the book-publishing division of InterVarsity Christian Fellowship, a student movement active on campus at hundreds of universities, colleges and schools of nursing in the United States of America, and a member movement of the International Fellowship of Evangelical Students. For information about local and regional activities, write Public Relations Dept., InterVarsity Christian Fellowship, 6400 Schroeder Rd., P.O. Box 7895, Madison, WI 53707-7895.

Note: All characters in this book are fictitious.

Cover illustration: John Walker

ISBN 0-8308-1351-9

Printed in the United States of America

Library of Congress Cataloging-in-Publication Data

Wicke, Ed.
    The muselings/by Ed Wicke.
      p.   cm.—(The Overton adventures)
   Summary: Three orphans are transported to the land of the Muselings and help free these kind, furry creatures from the power of wicked Queen Jess.
    ISBN 0-8308-1351-9
    [1. Fantasy. 2. Orphans—Fiction.] I. Title. II. Series: Wicke, Ed. Overton adventures.
   PZ7.W62656Mu 1991
   [Fic]—dc20   *91-13346*
                                           CIP
                                              AC

15	14	13	12	11	10	9	8	7	6	5	4	3	2	1
03	02	01	00	99	98	97	96	95	94	93	92	91		

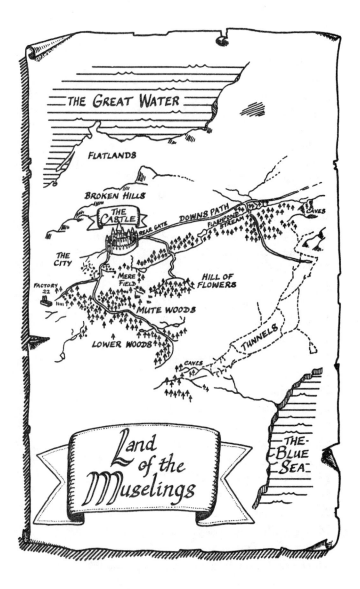

THE GREAT WATER

FLATLANDS

BROKEN HILLS

THE CASTLE

DOWNS PATH

REAR GATE

FLASHPOND STREAM

CAVES

THE CITY

MERE FIELD

HILL OF FLOWERS

FACTORY 22

MUTE WOODS

TUNNELS

LOWER WOODS

CAVES

Land of the Muselings

THE BLUE SEA

I

Beware the Dog

Summer was a season of crackling blue skies which shimmered in the sun and then burst into noisy thunderstorms just as the heat was heaviest. It was a summer when each day made you long for ice-cream, when twenty-pound watermelons were sold at the greengrocers, when grandmothers sipped iced drinks and said it had never been so hot as this, not even that July before the War when they had cooked minnows on the pavements.

Three hot scruffy children were splashing through Flashetts, seeking in that small wood beside the river Test some relief from the cruel sun and from the flies. There was a song about flies which children sang that year—about the blue biters and green stingers, black buzzers and nasty yellow ringers—and they were repeating it as they waved sticks fiercely before them, wandering along the riverbank. Rachel knew it best, having lived longest in the village, so she sang each line for the others to repeat.

'Buzz off, buzzers!' the others echoed her. She was ten, and the leader. Robert—eight—and Alice—six—were more than happy to chase along behind her. They were orphans, and lived in the crumbling orphanage close by the rectory. Of course, no one called it an 'orphanage'. It was known as the 'Children's Home', or just 'The Home'. The orphans called it The Black Hole, which might lead you to think they did not like it. In fact, they were quite pleased with it most days, just as their friends at school were mostly pleased with *their* homes.

Together with many other Overton children, they spoke a mixture of Hampshire and Cockney. They often lost an 'h' off the front of words, and usually lost any 't's in the middle of words. They also had the habit of stretching some vowels. A sentence such as 'Have you got a better chair?' might end up as something like ''Ave you go' a be''er chay-ah?' I can't of course put all this in writing whenever they speak—you will have to imagine it most of the time.

'Fly off, fliers!' Rachel called to them. 'Fly...,' they began. But then the dog started to bark. Alice, who was hot, and cross with the midges, shouted, 'Mad dog!' and began to run, as did the others.

At first it was only a game; they chased through the muddy paths, splashing joyfully, and dodged hot and breathless through the dangling brambles. Alice was soon well behind them; she had a twisted foot and could never keep up. To bring them back, she shouted, 'Mad dog ahead!'; they turned off the path, out of the woods altogether, and onto the track which led towards the church. Here they rejoined Alice and walked again, wiping the sweat from their eyes. They felt dreadfully hot as they came to the great oak. It stood near the road, opposite the churchyard.

Sitting beneath it, gasping at the heavy air, they checked the ground for ants. Then they watched the few cars move wearily up the hill towards the Downs, which shimmered in the hot distance. After a few minutes they heard the dog again.

The barking and crashing about continued for some time. The animal was moving towards them heavily. Although it was hidden in the woods, it was now near enough for them to hear its panting. Robert, who was least worried by the creature, was carelessly feeling the wrinkled trunk of the old tree.

'Look—one of them 'edgehogs!' he suddenly cried.

'So what?' Rachel replied impatiently. She was anxious

about the dog. There were now loud crackings as the beast leapt through the thick brush. Feelings of hot panic came upon her. Alice gripped her hand tightly. Silence fell for a few seconds; then they could hear heavy breathing, quite close now. The woods seemed to be watching them.

A branch moved in the scrub; something dark was pushing into the grass. Robert and Alice shouted at once. Alice cried something about a wolf; Robert about a door. Then, suddenly, there was a howling and leaping, and the three of them cowered against the tree. Something fell or broke or burst at their backs, and as darkness rose up before them a darkness opened behind them as well. Alice shouted once more—something about mother—and then they were falling helplessly. The barking died away in hollow bursts. There was silence, and a sudden warmth. Then nothing.

2

Creatures

Rachel awoke and found that opening her eyes made no difference to the darkness around her. 'Are you all right?' she asked softly.

'Yes.' The others spoke together.

Then Alice alone: 'There's something wrong with my foot. I can't move it.'

'I think I'm sitting on it.' Robert shifted stiffly to one side. 'Where are we?'

'Aren't we in the tree?' asked Rachel. 'I thought we fell inside it. You shouted something about a door. It seems like a dream now.'

'Didn't dream the dog,' Alice added in a low voice.

Rachel interrupted hurriedly. 'I was dreaming just now—before I woke. The same dream I had at home, I think it was. With the creatures and the castle and the flying things. Then—no, it's gone now. I can't remember.'

'Rob. Was there a hedgehog man?'

'Fink so. Or very like. Mixed in with the tree bark, clear as a drawing. And he was pointing—and there was a place like a door knob. I was feeling that when you two knocked me. Then we fell down.'

He peered at them through the dark. He could not see more than a dim variation in the blackness which must be Alice; Rachel was further away and could not be seen at all. They were sitting on a cool, flat surface. He stretched out an arm. It met a rough, grainy, curved wall which smelled of wood.

'We fell up,' Alice corrected him.

'Don't be silly.'

'We did—I watched when we fell in. The door went down, so we went up.'

'You can't fall up.'

'Can.'

'Stupid!'

Alice did not reply, but began to weep gently. Robert felt to his left and put his arm around her. 'Sorry, Ali. I didn't mean it. Come on, don't cry. We'll be all right.'

He heard Rachel stand up, feeling along the inside of the trunk with one hand and waving the other above her head so that she would not bang it. There was nothing above her.

'Let's be doing, then,' she said in her bravest voice. 'We'll get nowhere if we sit about on our bottoms. Be careful how you stand up; and let's hold hands. All right?' It was better now—holding on to one another. 'We ought to pray, really. You're supposed to when you're in trouble.'

Alice giggled. 'We're in sight of the church, anyway.'

'If we could see anything...look!'

Behind Rob they could now see the thinnest of lines of light which ran up from the floor and then right and down again, like the outline seen around the doorway of a lighted room. They pressed against the wall here, feeling about for a handle, but the cool surface was quite smooth. They pushed hard against it until they were hot and the air stuffy.

'We are stupid. The door opened in when we fell inside. Try to pull it, don't push!'

In vain they tried to force their fingernails into the cracks and pull the door towards them. Eventually, anger overtook them and they simply kicked at the trunk until their feet hurt.

Then Rachel shouted at it in exasperation, 'Open, you stupid thing!'

And it did, noiselessly.

A full light smote their eyes. They covered their sweaty

faces with grimy hands until they could see again without
pain. Anxiously, and curiously, they stepped out of the
trunk and gazed about them. They were not in the back of
Flashetts.

And yet it was not altogether different. To their left a
track passed up and over a rounded hill. About them were
trees (behind them the oak, looking much as it had previ-
ously); on the ground were flowers such as you might find at
home...or perhaps not. The colours were odd—they were
too vivid. Or was it just the sunlight? The weather was
warm rather than oppressively hot. Birds—heavens! What
bright feathers! Each one might be a kingfisher or a parrot!
Birds sang in the bushes and from the trees, and in this
place you would swear that the songs had words, and the
music a meaning. The children gaped at all this and turned
slowly from one side to another, staring at the strange
country. Behind them the door quietly shut itself.

Then they heard the voices: high and low voices joined in
song. It was not like any song they had heard: each voice
sang different words, and the song took the words and
blended them together into clear, soft music. It was as if
people were singing a discussion. Without thinking about
the possible danger, the children walked—then ran—to
find the source of the music. They did not consider whether
the singers might be savage and cruel. Somehow the music
itself reassured them.

They came to the side of the little clay road and stopped,
their hearts pounding. On the other side, in a circle, were a
dozen creatures. Each faced inwards, almost touching its
neighbours. None was clothed; all were covered in fur—
black, brown, grey or a coppery red. They stood about
Rachel's height on their two stubby legs, but you could see
that they would be equally at home on all fours. In our
world, you would have called them animals—until, that is,
you had seen their faces. Each furry face held eyes bright
and intelligent; each mouth was open in conversation or
song. A smile was to be seen here or there, and a twinkle
gleamed in the occasional eye.

'It's them!' Robert breathed. His eyes were large. He turned to Rachel. 'It's the hedge-'

But a sudden noise from the road scattered their thoughts. A trumpet sounded. Horses were galloping. A voice shouted, something about a queen. As the children turned this way, then that, they half glimpsed the hedgehog people vanishing quietly among the bushes. Only Alice saw one of them turn before going, and raise a hand—or paw— to the children as they stood startled by the road.

3

The Queen

A gong clanged. Down the red clay road, raising a fine dust, a procession came. The children stood, frozen by uncertainty. Their first impulse had been to run after the hedge-people, but the creatures had fled too quickly for them to follow. Then they had nearly turned back to the woods on their side of the road; but by now they had been seen. They waited, wide-eyed and worried.

A horse passed without checking its stride; the creature upon it, monkey-like, paid them no heed except to smile grimly at them. Next, two crocodile-creatures slithered— faster than you would think possible—along the smooth track, snapping at the air with their huge jaws. These eyed the children angrily, and one nipped at Rachel as they passed. After them came a parade of men who proudly stared before them, marching to time and swinging their arms precisely.

Lastly, came the Queen. She sat in an open carriage drawn by two horses. The carriage gleamed with gold, silver and bright jewels. She in her turn glittered in the strong sun. The children gaped at her. She seemed a fiery jewel which flamed in the sun and made all the woods look pale and dark in comparison. She shone with wealth.

With the raising of a bejewelled right hand, she caused the whole procession to stop. She looked down at the children with an indulgent smile. At once they felt a little more at ease, for to the eye, she was as human as they. She was also terribly beautiful, with brown hair falling softly to her waist and bright blue eyes set in a young face. She studied their grubby, ordinary faces for a long time, her smile continuing.

When at last she spoke, her voice was soft and friendly: 'I am so pleased you have come! Now let me see: you will be Rachel, will you not? And Robert, of course—and Alice? You are very welcome!' She gestured to them each in turn, and they nodded wonderingly as she told them their names.

She continued: 'And you are hot, thirsty and a little hungry? Come with me, and I will find you something from my kitchens.' The way she said 'kitchens' was so delicious that the children instinctively moved towards the coach— except for Robert, who said, 'What?' as he often did, being a little deaf (very deaf when he did not want to hear). 'What kittens?' he demanded.

The royal smile did not disappear, but the red lips thinned as the Queen repeated her invitation.

'Thank you,' said Rachel. 'We would be pleased to come.' She would have dropped a curtsey, but no one had taught her such things. So instead she gave a little nod of the head, then frowned at Robert and aimed a kick at his ankle as he passed her. He was a pain at times.

There was just room for them all in the carriage. The Queen kept up a bright conversation as they drove along the road, and managed to discover from them all what had happened to them that day, except for the glimpse they had caught of the hedge-creatures. Alice was just about to blurt out that they had run to the road because of the singing, when Rachel had pinched her and Robert had nudged Rachel who then elbowed him back (rather harder than the elbow she had received). When they had stopped shoving one another and whispering, the Queen asked again, innocently, 'So you made your way to the road because of the—?'

'Because of the noise,' Rachel inserted hastily. It was just true.

The Queen nodded and changed the subject. She was

very grand. She talked of fox-hunts, stag-hunts, balls, din-
ners, concerts, yachts and properties, machines and money.
They listened, overwhelmed, as she described her many
houses and lands.

'Over there,' said the Queen, sweeping a majestic arm to
the right, 'is a hill which I will take you to play upon. No
one but myself and a few chosen nobles are ever allowed
near it. Its summit is covered with a certain flower which
most people would give everything to have.' She laughed.
'And if they go there without permission, everything is what
they *lose!* The flowers are like diamonds a-growing; it would
not do for the common people to have them, or even to look
upon them...but you were telling me about the tree, and
the hedge-creatures you saw upon it. Why should you imagine that?'

'Robert saw some on a panel at the home—'

'How large is your residence—how many rooms and
towers does it have? And how many servants do you
employ? Is it as great as my castle?' She waved her arm
forwards, towards an immense, beautifully sprawling grey
stone building which squatted on the side of a green hill.
Below it, and continuing around the hill, a grey, smokey
city lay shimmering in the sharp sunlight.

'It's a little house,' said Alice sulkily.

'But there's old panels in it from the church, and the
creatures was on them,' added Robert.

The Queen looked at them keenly. 'How fascinating!' she
exclaimed. 'If you should find such things in my country, I
would be pleased to be shown them.'

'Are there hedgehog creatures here, then?' Alice asked
suddenly.

The Queen's eyebrows lifted slightly at this, but she
answered carelessly, 'Oh, there are creatures of all sorts in
my lands. Some of them are like the animals you describe:
we call them Muselings. But they are wild and dangerous.
A few have been tamed, and they are now in my zoos.
Those that live in the wood eat—but I do not wish to alarm
you.'

'We're not afraid of anything!' (This was an exaggeration—Alice was frightened of anything larger or fiercer than a spider.)

Reluctantly, it appeared, the Queen continued, 'It is said that the Muselings eat other creatures alive—especially children. Of course, I don't quite believe this myself, but we must accept what other people have seen.'

'Rubbish!' Robert exclaimed, then stopped and reddened.

The Queen appeared to take no offence, but commented mildly, 'You have spoken to them, then?'

The three retorted strongly that they had not, which was totally truthful. The Queen said no more, because they had just passed through the city gates, and she was nodding and waving graciously to the people who stopped by the roadside and removed their hats to her as the carriage approached. Most wore ordinary working clothes as they hurried about their business. From time to time, however, the carriage would pass what must be more prosperous citizens, and these wore fine silks, feathered hats, embroidered shawls and many items of jewellery. Yet they had this in common with the poorer people: none seemed to speak as they worked or travelled. Except for the distant sounds of machinery turning and grinding and thumping, it was uncommonly quiet.

Beyond the main street, in which they saw no other carriages, many a dull factory rose from the squat buildings which housed warehouses and shops. Smoke drifted from chimneys and settled on the rooftops; steams and vapours dissolved into the air. The grey city looked out of place in the green land.

But now they were leaving the factories as they rode up the hill towards the castle. There were trees again, and flowers by the roadside. Within a few minutes, they swung through the gate in the high stone wall which lay around the palace yard. The carriage drew to a halt before a great wooden door which was the front entrance to the castle. The children looked upwards and marvelled at the size of it:

there must be five or more storeys, each holding perhaps twenty rooms. A dark smoke came from chimneys at the rear—the kitchens, no doubt. They stepped down from the carriage, and started as a uniformed guard suddenly opened the door.

4

The Castle

The butler (for such he was) took the Queen's cape as she descended. Alice gave a surprised gasp when she saw the Queen standing upright, for her majesty was of a great height. She was tall as a door, and broad-shouldered as a man. Her bright, tight red dress flowed from shoulders to the ground, sparkling with gems. It showed her full figure as she arched back to gaze up at the turrets of her castle. The sun was falling fast and the Queen's shadow darted far across the lawns that lay before the palace. She sighed with pleasure, and placed a gentle hand on Rachel's shoulder.

'All this—do you see it? It is the Queen's and hers alone. She who is Queen may stretch out one hand, even one small finger, and all pleasure—all the good things of life—will then run to satisfy her beckoning. The Queen's...a child like yourself might some day be a Queen.'

Rachel said nothing. The Queen's lands were nothing to her compared with her daydreams of a small back garden of a small home, with its swing and its plot of peas and sweet corn and its bright poppies. Robert said nothing either; he was squatting to look under the carriage. It gave a very bouncy, though smooth ride. Why was that? Was it the long curved metal bars which ran between the axles that the wheels hung upon? And—yes—they were rubber wheels, so there must be a factory somewhere making rubber. This world was very like the old one in many ways.

'And how old are the three of you?' asked the Queen as

she led them into the palace, and then into a high, light room with a table in it as long as a tennis court is wide.

Rachel thought hard and replied, 'Twenty-four.'

'Oh, but—' the Queen began, puzzled. 'Surely—that is, how can you be so old?'

'We're not!' exclaimed Robert, who had guessed the joke. 'You asked how old the three of us were. Six, eight and ten make twenty-four!'

'I see,' the Queen replied mildly. She did not join their laughter, but commented kindly enough, when Alice had finished giggling, 'You will find a place to wash through that door' (pointing to the far wall) 'and when you return we shall have some food. I expect you are famished.' She left the room.

The walls were all panelled in light wood, and the floors were also wooden. They were dark and waxy and just right for sliding upon. Rachel rushed after Robert and dragged him back from an attempt to skate from one side to the other.

'We'll get in trouble, dummy!' she whispered urgently in his good ear.

She glanced guiltily about the hall. There were pictures on the walls, perhaps of the Queen's relatives. All were of great size and impressive features. It was not a comfortable room; you felt that the pictures watched you all the time. There was worse to come because there were also pictures in the wash-rooms and loos. Robert turned these around so that they all faced the wall.

Back in the hall, they found the table had been covered with a silky red cloth. This in turn was covered with all manner of fruits, salads, breads, cheeses, nuts and delicious puddings. There was no meat at all, but this was not missed. They ate happily and rather greedily, aware from time to time that their manners were not those which the many pictures were accustomed to view from their perches on the walls.

The Queen joined them after some minutes and ate daintily and sparsely. Rachel could not help but reflect that this large, strong woman must normally eat more substantial meals.

'I could of course send you home immediately,' the Queen was saying as she chose a pear. 'But time runs differently here. Were you to return now, you would find that only a brief moment had passed in—you called it Flashetts, I believe?'

'The dog would still be there,' whispered Alice unhappily.

'I fear it would, little one. You see, it would not be a responsible act on my part if I were to permit your return— not yet, that is. By tomorrow evening, a minute or two would have passed by, like a cloud drifting across a sleepy summer sky. But of course, it would be better still to remain here for several days—would you not think so, Robert?' She spoke in a confidential, persuasive manner which entreated the three of them to trust her.

Robert nodded, his mouth too full of chocolate and almond mousse to say anything. Alice was looking dreamily at the ceiling, seeing in the leafy brown patterns there the hot brush of Flashetts and a dark creature which lurked in the shadows. Rachel frowned at them both, exasperated. She wanted to go back as soon as possible; but really— those two! She supposed it was because they had no real home to return to.

What was happening back in Overton? She imagined, with amusement, the short, wide form of Mrs Welter searching the village for her; the Rector giving out their names at church; the other children wishing gloomily that they too had escaped. Perhaps Mrs Welter would just mark them absent for a night. In any case, they would catch it when they got back. Kitchen duty for a week, probably. If only the Queen were right: a few minutes would not matter. But...'I'm not sure,' she said.

The Queen, sitting on Rachel's right, leaned close and spoke reassuringly. 'You can trust me. I will see that your parents receive you back before they know you have been away.' And she added, this time speaking to Alice, 'You'll be home to your mother and father very soon—by their time, that is.'

Alice's eyebrows shot up, and she reddened quickly. Robert looked the other way.

Slightly flustered, the Queen began to describe to them the delights of hunting. 'The Royal Hounds, now—you must pay a visit to them. They can tear a fox apart before you could say the alphabet, you know—and such noses! They can track deer for absolutely miles, and then have enough strength to chase them to a standstill and pull a stag down for a kill.' She held a peach in her hand as she spoke and suddenly broke it neatly in two with a twist of the fingers.

'How d'you know our names?' Robert asked suddenly. Somewhere, deep in his thoughts, this question had been brooding.

'It is in the Words,' she said, ignoring the mystified looks which followed this statement. 'But that is something adults alone can discuss. You will have to accept my word for it. "A boy and two sisters, young and old"—that is what it says.'

Alice suddenly laughed aloud. 'You must have read the wrong page then. We're none of us related!'

The Queen's eyes flashed, and she choked on a wedge of peach.

5

The Message

Their room was high, large and square. Three beds lay in a row to the right of the door, their headboards against the same wall. A kind-looking, dumpy woman had shown them the chests and wardrobes they could use, where already had been gathered beautiful clothes made for small princes and princesses.

They sat together on the middle bed, with their backs to the door. They were looking across the room and out of the large low window, studying the road they had travelled a few hours before. Where the orange clay of the road disappeared at the horizon, small white clouds could be seen gathering and darkening in the red sunset. A wind was shivering through the branches of the far trees; a storm would come with the fall of night.

'This is some adventure!' Robert whispered.

'I want to go back.'

'We'll go home soon, dear,' Rachel comforted Alice. 'The Queen said we could.'

'I don't trust her a sausage,' observed Robert. 'She's planning something and we're just part of the plan. Look how she nearly had a fit when she discovered we weren't from the same family.'

Rachel, cradling Alice in her lap, shook her head at him vigorously. She pointed to Alice with her free hand, meaning that they must try not to upset her. But Alice herself joined in.

'She's a wicked lady.'

'Alice—you don't know that!'

'Would you like an apple, my dear?' Alice imitated the Queen's voice while pretending to be the wicked Queen of Snow White. The others laughed. 'Wait and see. Why did you all say you wanted to stay if you're so keen on getting home?'

'You was the one afraid of the dog. You knocked us through the tree—remember?' Robert insisted.

'That's nothing to do with it! And I didn't, so there. I'm no more afraid than you. I'd go back now.'

They had to break from the argument because Alice had dropped off to sleep and was about to fall from the bed. Wearily they woke her, and then they all changed into the heavy red cotton nightshirts that had been provided for them. There were no washbasins in the room, and no toothbrushes in any case, so they went without. They did not mind at all. At the home you brushed and washed several times a day; this was like a holiday. Turning out the light, they said their prayers and were soon asleep between cool, soft sheets.

Alice awoke from a dream about the home. They had been sitting in the garden, feeding birds with crumbs. Then a crow had come and driven away the other birds. It stood before them on the grass, its mouth wide. They threw bread to it, but the bird was not satisfied. It came closer and closer, cawing at them angrily and snapping its beak. As it approached, it grew until it was as large as Alice, then as great as a house. It began to peck at Robert, while she cried and threw rocks at it. It turned aside, and tilted its dark greedy eye to her. The head stretched down, beak open...

She was sitting on her bed. The covers were thrown upon the floor, and through the half-dark her pillow could be seen at the foot of her bed. Moonlight sifted murkily through the crossbeams of the window, through which came a distant rumbling of dark thunder. Her arms were crossed above her head to ward off the dream-creature. She was sweating, and terribly thirsty.

The others were asleep. She shook Rachel, who turned over and muttered in her sleep, 'Yes, yes, that's right. Three and two make....'

She would have to go and get a drink by herself. As she crossed the room, she awoke fully and remembered that they were not at the home, but in the palace in—in where? They hadn't asked the name of the country. Never mind, she could find the bathroom where they had washed before tea. She opened the door gently. The corridor was dark and noiseless. Down the passage she tiptoed, then turned right onto the stairs. Down, bearing right again at the bottom, and left to the dining hall, through to the bathroom.

The pictures were still facing the wall. She shivered. If she turned one around, would she find its eyes looking at her, and moving? She drank quickly and ran out again into the hall. After that, she followed her course back towards the room.

She had walked for almost a minute before she realised that she was lost. Surely that statue had not been there before, if it were a statue—its eyes were so real. She panicked and ran along another hallway, then turned left and right again. She paused. No one had followed her. Heart pounding, she set off to find the stairs. Why, there they were—just to the right.

Up, along, left and—lost again. She halted, leaning against a door—and almost screamed as a voice spoke, not a yard from her, on the other side of the door.

It was a low, growling voice. 'There was no mistake, I tell you! The timing was right, plain as plain—plain as the nose on your face, I say!'

'But they are so young—far too young!' The voice that replied was like the Queen's, but not exactly so. It had a whining, hard sound and a metalic coldness like the inside of a freezer. 'If the boy had been a little older—even a year or two—or the older girl sillier, I might have done something with them. Can you be sure you are right?'

The first voice was now angry, but formal and precise. 'If you believe that you can do my job better than I, please say so directly. I tell you that the signs were all present, and the Words bear me out. And who else among your servants has the courage to do as I have done? I sat in view of their poisonous church day and night, waiting my chance to bring them here; if you would suffer that, take my place!'

'Please do not take offence. I do not question your courage. But there is a problem with the Words—do you not see? It is not right that the three do not come from the same family. Unless we have read wrongly, that is. After all, the Words were written for the creatures, not for us. We're only guessing.'

'I believe you need only persuade one to trust you, and we will have accomplished everything.'

'Not everything. And it would be better if I could persuade them all to join us. It is only that—'

Suddenly there was silence, and the first person could be heard to sniff loudly. 'What's this, then?' he cried.

Alice began to creep away. Her legs were weak as a jelly and she could hardly breathe.

The other voice shot out imperiously, 'Stay, Snarl! No one leaves me without my permission!'

As Alice turned a corner and began to run, she heard a stiff, jumbled argument from the room. As she reached the bottom of the stairs, a door was slapped open and something growled as it flung itself down the corridor.

She turned left, right and left; up some stairs (thank heavens, the right ones), then, almost weeping, flew to their room as quietly as she could. She threw herself and the bedclothes back upon the bed and lay gasping for air, trembling violently. Within a minute there was a sound of stealthy feet, then a hoarse snuffling. She heard the doorknob rattle and turn. She forced herself not to look, and breathed as normally as possible. The door opened and someone stood within the doorway.

Suddenly another voice cried, 'And what are you doing up here, then?' It was the maid. The door closed. There was an argument, and the maid could be heard shouting roughly at someone who stamped down the stairs. Then silence.

Alice burst into tears and within a few minutes had cried herself to sleep. She had to wipe her face on the pillow because she had dropped her handkerchief on the stairs.

6

Church

They were awakened by soft but repeated knocking. It was late morning—the sunshine that crowded through the windows was angled sharply down onto the floor. As the door opened, a voice—the maid's—reminded them where they were.

Cereals, toast and milk on patterned gold trays were brought by two women. These did not speak but stood still as wooden dolls, solemnly watching the children eat. The maid however chattered pleasantly, asking cheerily whether they had slept well, and describing the weather they would have that day. It would be blustery, indeed, but warm and not too wet. They would have a good day for walking, or riding, or games.

Then when she had removed the breakfast articles, she nodded to them brightly, whispered something to Alice, and then trotted out.

'Ali?' asked Rachel.

Alice had paled and sat with her little white hands clenched together. 'I just remembered a bad dream.' She told them what she remembered of the night; but it was a vague and wispy story, like a watery mist fading in the sunlight. The maid had said she had heard her shouting in her sleep, and was she all right now? 'It seemed so real at the time—I even thought I could smell the creature at the door.'

Robert raised his eyes to the ceiling to show what he

thought of the story. Neither he nor Rachel had woken, and they would have done so if anything had really happened.

'We'll be late if you two spend the morning telling stories. Rachel will say next that she dreamt of the flying thing again,' Robert muttered. He had already begun to pull on the clothes that had appeared by their beds, replacing their own clothes which the servants had apparently taken with the breakfast trays.

Rachel helped Alice into the red dress set out for her, and found to her surprise that it fitted very well indeed—as well as the golden dress fitted her own lanky body. (Someone with a fine eye for shape must have spent yesterday sewing them.) While they laced stiff leather shoes, they discussed the day before them. They would go with the Queen: they would explore the castle—they would perhaps go out for a walk. Then they would persuade the Queen to send them home. At this last word, Alice began to weep.

The others pulled her over to the high windows, from which they examined the countryside. There was the road they had travelled on, to the left; to the right was the hill of flowers, and beyond it another hill which rose gently, then steeply, then precipitously. Bare rock gleamed from its summit, catching the yellow sunlight and tossing it back in shimmers of blue and grey. It would be hot today, whatever breezes there were; hot even as the unsheltered meadows around Flashetts. Already, flies were buzzing here as there, great green-headed creatures which seem to inhabit every world, as if they alone knew the secret passageways from one world to another.

There was a noise of metal clanging on metal—a gong perhaps—and the three turned with a sigh. Alice wiped her face on her sleeve.

'Time for church, I s'pose,' Rachel breathed unenthusiastically. They went along the passage and down the stairs slowly, peering into the dark corridors which they crossed. As they turned the final flight of steps, Rachel noticed a patterned handkerchief upon the carpet and automatically tidied it into her pocket. A clear voice called

them, and they saw near the dining hall the Queen awaiting
them, dressed in green velvet and wearing a fur stole and
hat. She clutched a tiny black book and carried a black
purse. Smiling at them, she held out her hands. One at a
time they came forward and were kissed upon the forehead.
Rachel recalled miserably that they had none of them
washed that morning.

'My own little family! I trust you slept well?' Her eyes
sought theirs, and they tried at first to return her gaze, but
she was too great a lady for them and they soon shyly
looked down. 'Come now! Rested and ready for a day of
pleasure? Tell me that you are, please!'

'Yes, ma'am,' they responded, to please her; and then,
because she was such a great and awesome and lively
person, they felt themselves growing excited and they spoke
all at once: 'Are we going to that hill?'

'Will we see the palace—the horses too?'

'Did you say there was treasure?'

She laughed gaily, holding up her hands for silence.
'Everything in its own time, please! First the service; then
the pleasure (no, not treasure, I fear, Robert); then the
homecomings for those who are ready for home. Though I
should be desolate if you find me such a poor hostess as to
be thinking of home already.' She gave them a teasing look
and a little laugh, clear and sweet as a bell. 'Come along,
then! Heads up and eldest first!'

She led them to what she called the 'Sanctuary'. It was
large, stony and ugly. Within it, the air was damp and cold
between the many pillars, and the light was dingy. But
beautiful stained-glass windows told many incomprehens-
ible stories in blue, green, yellow and red pictures.

They did not remember much about the service after-
wards, except that it had been long and dull and full of
words they did not understand. Rachel had peered up at the
ceiling, wondering why adults seemed to like miserable
church services. Not that the ones she went to in Overton
were like that. Elias Jones, the old Rector, made the place
come alive even on cold winter mornings. Sometimes you

could imagine it was Palm Sunday again, with the children
throwing down palm branches before the donkey and
shouting 'Hosanna!'

Alice was giggling, bent over the pages of a black book
which had been in the pew when they had arrived there.
The others glanced to the left and saw with relief that the
Queen was asleep. They looked at the page which Alice
indicated. It read:

Wisdom of Ed. Chapter 1 of the Words.

(1) Early to bed, early to rise: for a child it is good, but for a
worm unwise.

(2) A king has to wash behind his ears just like anyone else.
True royalty is a matter of the heart alone.

They read no further, because the service had come to an
end, and the Queen awoke. They followed her down the
aisle, and were suddenly in a sunshine which slapped hotly
at their eyes as they left the dark church.

'Children!' They were beckoned by a muscled arm emerg-
ing from royal furs and soft velvet. 'I wish you to meet the
commander of my armies. Lord Lrans—these are the dear
children I met by Mute Woods.' She told him their names
and then hurried off.

They nodded to him as he nodded proudly to them.
What a face he had—as backward, complicated and aristo-
cratic as his name! It was mostly brown beard—or fur,
since in this land you could hardly say which was which—
and from this emerged a broad, flat nose over a thin mouth
and sharp, small chin. His tiny hazel eyes (with a gold-
rimmed monocle on the left one) were bright and steady, as
if like a snake he were given to careful and long observation.
His teeth showed when he smiled: they were bright and
small.

'Pleased-to-meet-you,' he said quickly in a low gravelly
voice. He looked them over severely for a long minute.
'Don't know if you like hunting; if so, we can arrange a few
outings. Ride a horse? Ought to learn. The best test of a

civilised man is to see if he can hunt on a thundering fast mount and then have the stomach to be in on the killing.'

'I'm sorry, we've never—'

'You could have a couple of my creatures to ride.' His voice had now become angry. 'Good for hound meat, and not much else. Couldn't hold their tongues; well, someone can do it for them. You can keep a civil tongue in your heads, I s'pose?'

'*Three* tongues—' Robert began, gleefully correcting the minor error. The commander of all the Queen's armies stared balefully at them in furious silence, and then abruptly walked away.

Rachel whistled under her breath. 'I like that! Listens well, don't he?'

Robert bowed low to Alice. 'Pleesmeecha,' he said. 'Like killing things? Only decent way to live, killin' things!'

'My Lord Lrans,' Rachel pleaded to him, 'I am but a simple duchess. Pray permit me to learn wisdom from your furry lips, and teach me in the fair art of mangling animals.'

Alice had folded her hands solemnly and was copying the minister's quavering voice when the others poked her into silence. A sour-faced lady (one of the choir) had sidled up quietly and was suddenly upon them.

'*She* wishes,' (and by the way she bowed her head devoutly at '*She*', they knew who '*She*' was) 'that you should ride with her to the Hill. It is my honour to take you to the stables.' The choir lady spoke sweetly, with that especially careful kindliness that people use when they are trying to appear friendly. Then a sly look came into her eyes and it spread quickly over the rest of her face.

Looking about her, she continued, '*She* would not be pleased to hear all that I have heard. You are fortunate that only I heard you. Your words are safe with me. But remember that I could tell if I wished! Not that I would—but it would be my duty to tell, and I must have some compensation for my trouble.'

She said the word 'compensation' as if it were a particularly nice box of chocolates, and Robert believed for several moments that this was indeed what she wanted.

'Now—if you were to bring me some flowers—no, not so much as that, but just one small flower, the smallest one even: one flower from the hilltop. Then I would forget all you said—I promise that. Without a small present such as one such flower, I would remember for a long time.'

She swept away, and they miserably scurried behind her, past several large sheds and paddocks to a stable which stood not far from the kitchens. A smell of dogs, horses, wet earth and boiled cabbage salted the warm air.

A few yards before the stables, they passed a foul and tiny yard in which two horses were tethered. There was food and water before them, but their jaws were tied so that they could not eat or drink. As the children passed, one horse—a chestnut mare with a white blaze on her nose and forehead—whinnied. It was a hoarse rattling sound which told of many days without water.

'Why—' began Rachel.

The woman tossed her head. 'Mind your own business.'

She turned and gave them a hard, cruel glance, then walked on as before, saying crisply, 'They said no worse than you've said, bear that in mind. They only got what they had coming to them.'

7

Ponies

The stable of the royal horses was itself something of a palace. There were large barred windows, turrets, high doors, great bolts, and a heavy iron gate. A guard stood just within this gate, flicking at the flies which burred and bumbled lazily in the mid-morning heat. He straightened as the group came within his sight, then nodded to the choir lady and stood to one side. He renewed his battle with the flies, and stood muttering gently to himself as the children passed.

The choir lady sniffed at him. 'Three ponies, Mr Hector, if you please.' Her voice was sniffy, too. (Well-bred people don't criticise, they just sniff at you with their nose or their voice and make you feel small—which is just as bad as the ordinary way of being nasty.) Mr Hector snorted, just like a horse, pawed the ground a little (just like a horse), and began to explain in a wheezy sort of way that he'd not been told about this, and he was to guard the door, not fetch ponies. But he did fetch three black ponies because the well-bred choir lady stood and sniffed at him until he did what she'd asked.

'Of course, you'd like 'em saddled, I suppose?' He directed this question to the children. He smiled as he spoke in his hoarse voice, and tossed his head a little. His hair had a long black fringe which hung across his forehead until he flipped it with a little flick of the head, when it fell upon his right ear and then slipped round slowly until it came over his forehead again. He winked mischievously at the three with his head turned so that the choir lady could not see it, and gave them a rope to hold each. At the end of the ropes were ponies, small to large, and each pony pawed the ground like Mr Hector and tossed its head, flicking its forelock onto its ears.

The lady left once she had reminded the children about the flowers, in an urgent whisper this time because Mr Hector was somewhere about, finding tack for the animals. The three stood in the wide passage near the gate, eyeing the ponies who in their own way eyed the children, which for a pony involves looking, smelling, rubbing up against, and nibbling upon in a delicate manner, as the children now discovered.

'Getting acquainted, then?' Mr Hector plodded along the passageway to them. He handed each child a bridle, stopping to give each pony a long, horsey scratch. 'Doc...Grumpy...Sleepy.... Now be good boys—no bites, bucks, runaways, kicks or sidescrapes. Right?'

'What's a skyscrape?' asked Robert, looking doubtfully at Grumpy.

'Oh that—that's uhm, *side*scrape, yes, that's when he comes to something like a tree or a wall and walks just by it, you know. But so close as to—to rub *you* up against it. It's a pony trick. Horses too, of course. But ponies probably invented it.'

'Do you have seven ponies, then, Mr Hector?' Rachel put in very quickly. She had been making guesses and wanted to speak it before the others thought of it.

He bowed to her. 'Just call me Heck, my lady.' They giggled.

'And you are—of horse—of—of course—correct. Seven ponies, the seven—'

'Dwarfs!'

'Compared with a horse, a pony is a dwarf, you know—or midget. But the Seven Midgets, it's not even a fairy tale. Though we could write one, you know—if we had time, that is.'

He showed them how to fit the bridles. They were surprised that the ponies readily opened their mouths to accept the cold metal bits ('snaffle bits' Heck called them), which they then chomped on as pleasurably as any dog worrying an old bone. They held the reins while he stumped away to find saddles.

'Watch Grumpy!' he called down the passageway. 'Or he'll be off.'

Grumpy shook his head as if to disagree. Robert clenched the reins and studied the black animal who showed no sign of being 'off'. Heck brought the saddles, and they followed his instructions for fitting them. He leaned against the gate, watching the three struggle with saddle blanket, stirrups and girth strap. ('Think of it as a belt—but one which goes about the chest. Now where's your chest? No, that's your midriff. Higher—gracious, poor Sleepy—you'll squeeze him in half if you pull like that. Firm and slow. Fasten the buckle. Right?')

At last the ponies were prepared, and the children stood panting. Heck laughed at them.

'You'll do,' he said, 'but it's not so easy with horses. Done all right for learners.' He rubbed his head thoughtfully and studied them from under the hair that had fallen back across his eyes.

'You may need to know how to saddle and bridle a horse. Come, come along here. Bring the boys.' He led them to a room in which hung saddles, bridles, halters and so on. The salty, soapy smell of leather stung their noses. He touched a few items, and made a game of their learning the use of each.

'Next time we come—' began Robert, when Heck held up a finger to his ear. They listened. A strong, royal voice could be heard outside the stables.

'If I'm not here,' he said, 'look under the gate itself. I'll leave a key. Quick now—she's waiting.'

The Queen was on a great silver stallion, speaking with a servant—probably a groom, because she seemed to be giving orders about the feeding of horses. Or rather, not feeding them. As Alice led Sleepy around the gate, she heard: 'Not a thing—no water, no food. And don't clean their stalls. No—on second thoughts, leave them in the yard. But tie them tight. Or el—hello dear! Come on then. I'm waiting for you!'

She sent the groom away with a wave of a hand and then leapt gracefully from her horse. She showed them how to mount and apologised nicely for not being there to help them 'dress the ponies', as she called it. She remounted her bright horse, who had been eyeing the ponies doubtfully, as if he could not believe that they were going to come with him. Grumpy snorted at him in a welcoming sort of way. The stallion lifted his chin, sniffed as if he were the choir lady, and looked in the opposite direction. Ponies were beneath him.

The Queen's saddle had panniers on either side, clad in silver. She slapped them to call the children's attention to them, and cried gaily, 'Lunch!' They set off, at a walk and then a trot.

Riding was more difficult and more unusual than they had imagined. Ponies have a short, quick stride at all speeds, and bounce you up and down mercilessly. Nearly half an hour of jarring and bumping passed before they suddenly discovered the ponies' rhythm and began to move with the willing creatures. They found that it was better not to concentrate on the movements of their mounts—this seemed to make it easier to ride smoothly.

The Queen rode superbly, with a natural grace and an effortless, flowing sway of her hips. Her legs clung to the tall muscular horse, who was straining to be given his head so that he could show these pesky ponies how to run. Suddenly she cried loudly to him and he leapt away, bearing her with great thrusting strides across a field at full gallop. Her hair streamed behind her. She leant forward in her bright saddle, the sunlight catching her jewelled cloak and making her path like that of a lightning slash through the field.

'Whew! She can ride, can't she?'

'On a broom-stick, too, I bet.'

'Robert!'

'That's rude, Bob.'

'Sorry.'

She had halted at the edge of the wood which was hard against the right-hand side of their path here, and was staring into its cool depths as if she had seen something within it. After several seconds, she wheeled her horse about and returned to them at a fast canter. Both she and the stallion were breathing hard. She smiled broadly. 'Come then! You did not follow me! Look—let your body sit back into your saddle and make your legs drop a little further down. Pull your shoulders back. Good! Now loosen the reins a little. Give a little squeeze with your legs—and go!'

The ponies took off with a jolt and a jump. Then they settled down, their little legs moving fast and rhythmically. Down a gentle hill they rushed, and across a flat meadow. Alice was laughing, and couldn't stop. Robert looked distressed but held on grimly and did not try to slow Grumpy. Rachel was beginning to enjoy riding and was thinking so. Then Doc stumbled, swerved, swerved back. The ground came up, or so it seemed, and Rachel found herself on it. She was flustered and a little dizzy. Doc was twenty paces on, slowing and then standing still.

Embarrassed but not hurt, she scrambled over to Doc, who was grazing happily. He tossed his head at her as if to say that he was sorry. Or was it a look of pure mischief he gave her? Anyway, he allowed her to catch him and remount. She prepared to follow the others. Then she remembered: she must check the girth first. She scrambled down again and tightened the strap a little.

'You'll do.'

She jumped and turned around. Then she remounted Doc grumbling, 'Silly girl! Hearing things.'

The others were waiting at the end of the field. She rode up to them sheepishly. Alice was concerned; Robert was quiet; the Queen was amused.

'Poor girl! You flew and you landed with a bump! Do not be ashamed—I saw him stumble; it was not your fault. And you leapt up again quite creditably. No bones broken? Then the experience will do you good. All the best riders have fallen many times.'

They continued at a walk.

Alice asked, 'Did you ever fall off?'

The Queen considered. Her thinking went on for some time; Robert was sure that she had forgotten the question.

'Did you?' he repeated loudly.

She looked at him narrowly and he realised that the repetition was not welcome. He felt that she thought him very impolite. He reddened and slowed Grumpy so that he was riding a little behind her. She turned to Alice. 'Yes, little one. Three times, once badly. I broke an arm. But that was long ago.'

'Have you ridden a long time, then?'

'Oh—ages. Centuries!' She waved an arm high in the air. Robert copied her from behind. Rachel saw it and sniggered. Without turning around, the Queen remarked coldly, 'Do not do that again, young man.'

Robert slowed his horse even more. 'Sorry,' he muttered.

'Really centuries?'

'Millennia.'

'Rachel,' Robert whispered. 'Why did she say millipedes when Alice said centipedes?'

'Wash your ears, silly.'

'All right. Where's the water?'

Alice was still puzzling. 'You never told us your name. Don't you have one?'

The Queen laughed. Rachel and Robert laughed, then Alice too. Rachel said, 'Of course she has a name, baby— but you must call a Queen "Your Majesty".'

'You may call me Jess. As a special favour. But not when anyone else is about.'

They were climbing steadily, and were nearing the top of the hill which Jess had shown them on the first day. There was a small paddock about a hundred yards before the trees which marked the summit. Jess rode to it, dismounted, and motioned for the three to do likewise. They led the animals into the paddock and closed the gate. Removing saddles and bridles, they hung these on the fence. Jess carried the saddle-bags to a low, spreading tree. They feasted.

There was some magic about her packing of the panniers. First came hot crusty bread and butter, with strawberry jam. Then cool cider. Then salad, cheeses, puffy crispy savouries, pretzels and pickled onions. Then soft swirly chocolate ice cream cornets. And a slice each of melon. Alice kept picking up the bags and studying their insides. There were still items at the bottom, but they were never brought out: everyone was too full. They sat, ate, sighed and dozed.

8

The Hill

Rachel woke because Robert was muttering. 'Of course—of horse we will. Seven times three...twenty-one and three to carry. One to lose...take you with us...oh—ow!'

Rachel had pinched him. 'Wake up, Sleepy!'

'Go 'way, Grumpy. Stop it. I said we'd take...oh—Rach...I thought Grumpy was biting me.'

'You were dreaming.'

He opened his mouth as if to say something. Then he sat back against the tree and watched the ponies in the paddock, intently. Rachel went to wake Alice.

The Queen was in the paddock, examining her horse's hooves. When she saw the children moving about, she hailed them. 'This way. We walk to the top—up along the path!'

It was painful at first. They ached from riding, in muscle and joint. She laughed at them. 'It will be worse tonight, and worse yet tomorrow! But you have made a start. I do believe you will be fine riders. Worthy of a royal mount, one day.'

'Why are we walking?'

'The horses would not come up here.'

'Why not?'

In answer, Jess shaded her eyes from the sun, which lay above and to the left of the summit. She indicated a shadow beyond a belt of trees. 'Do not be afraid. But stay close to me.'

Her request that they be not afraid immediately had the opposite effect: a cold dread fell upon them. Alice clung to Rachel. Robert moved near to the Queen who, surprisingly, placed her arm around his shoulders. As they approached the trees which ringed the hill as a spikey green crown, the shadow moved. It was very large. Then they entered the wood and lost sight of it.

It was when they passed again into the sunlight that the shadow took shape. It was bird-like and rat-like, blood-red and sharp-clawed. It stood high as a large shed and long as two cars. It had fur, not feathers; a beak which was curved and sharp; eyes which stared coldly. Rachel suffered a stab of recognition. She had seen those eyes in dreams.

'Crow! Down!' cried the Queen. The creature's icy stare did not falter or even flicker, but it slowly lowered itself to the ground, spread its wings flat upon the earth, and nodded its head in obeisance. The large black eyes glittered with malice.

'Go!' Her eyes held the creature's gaze for a long moment, as if to tell it more than her few words. It nodded again, then suddenly rose into the air, fanning the three with a strong-smelling wind. It rose quickly and disappeared towards the white road.

Jess smiled round at the children who were clasped together like the petals of a flower closing for the night. 'Do not fear, I said! He is not beautiful; he is even dangerous; but he has a good heart, and he is mine! My very own, my poppet. He will not harm you or any that I love. And since you wish names, little one (she knelt and patted Alice's head), his name is Ahab. And he is a very old man. Millipedes old, Robert!'

They stood unhappily upon the wide green summit. The creature's shadow seemed to stay upon the hill. Yet Jess laughed playfully and teased them at their fear of her 'little bird'. They made an effort to laugh as well, as she led them into the short grass and showed them the flowers.

'Silverline, that is their name. No! Do not pick them! The

Queen alone may pluck a flower. Alice, did you hear me?'
she insisted.

Alice halted, her fingers already tightening about a stem.
The smell of the flowers made them giddy. It was as if a
sharp lemon tang had been mixed with the softness of peach
scent. The flowers themselves were indeed bright like silver
when looked at from above; then if you looked through
them towards the sky, the sunlight sparkled through them
as though they were jewels. When you stood and regarded
them waving in the cool breeze, they were a sea of twinkling
stars—now bright as mirrors, now scattering light like
diamonds. Alice was bewildered and enchanted by them.
She reluctantly let the flower slip from her grasp.

'Why?' she asked—and then added hurriedly, 'Please
tell us why we can't pick them.'

'You may of course pick as many as you wish—if you ask
and if I allow it. But ordinarily no one may take a flower
from here. That is why Ahab lives on the hill. He is the
guardian of the flowers.'

Robert gave her a funny look. He blurted out, 'But that
lady wanted us to bring one back to her.' He paused,
embarrassed.

The Queen appeared not to have heard. 'Let's play a
little game,' she suggested. 'If you girls will go to the other
side of this little field, and Robert and I stay here, we will
pick five flowers each. But you must try to find the biggest
and best on your side, as we will on ours. Who picks the
best flowers may keep them.'

With a cheer, the girls ran quickly across the field. Jess
called to them to take their time. In ten minutes they would
compare posies.

'Now, young man—for man indeed you are—come tell
me about this. We will have a discussion, for I think we
understand one another.'

She drew Robert close to her side, and he unwillingly
repeated what the choir lady had said. She questioned him
closely until she was satisfied that he had not misheard the

lady. Then she smiled sweetly. 'We must take her a flower, then, must we not?'

'But—please, Jess, why does she want them so much?'

'Because they can make a person live for ever—or nearly for ever.' She said it in a matter-of-fact voice, as though it were of no importance.

But the thought took away Rob's breath. 'That's incredible!' he choked out.

'You would like to live for ever? Then you may keep a flower as well.' Again, her voice was steady—but her eyes could not hide a sudden gleam. Robert became uneasy. He began to wish Rachel was there, or someone—like Heck, or the mother he'd never had. He began to think about wanting not to be an orphan, but to live in a family.

'Maybe,' he muttered. Her eyes were fixed on his, and he looked bashfully at the grass which came to just above his ankles. As though she knew his thoughts, she murmured: 'Then you could live with me, and I could look after you. Then when you were full-grown, you could look after me. A queen needs a king, you know—someone to help her.' She held a flower out to him. He did not take it. Something in his mind did not like the feel of all this. Her words—so good, so gentle, yet he was unsettled in his mind.

She sighed and added the flower to her own collection. She gave a slight sniff. He looked up and saw her wipe an eye, turning away as if to stop him from seeing her cry.

'Sorry, Jess—really, I am. I didn't mean to upset you. It's so kind of you—'

'Let's not speak of it.' Her voice was sad, but forgiving. 'Give me a small kiss to say that we are friends.'

He hesitated. If he were to be honest, he would say that they were not yet friends at all. But it was so hard to refuse her. She was making him feel mean and guilty. Surely it wouldn't be wrong to make her feel better by pretending he liked her and trusted her? It was only a little lie, after all.

She saw his hesitation. Her voice came again, this time with an edge of annoyance to it, 'At least give me your hand on it!'

He held to her his left hand, which was nearest. This displeased her, and she took instead his right. She held it tight between her two hands, then pressed it to her lips. Her lips were warm. When she released his hand, it was tingling. He blushed, and in his mind his hand seemed to burn with his embarrassment.

They began now to pick flowers and had just time to gather theirs when the girls returned; and so of course Rachel's and Alice's bunches were far superior. Rachel had spent most of her time helping Alice to choose a posy, and Alice certainly had the nicest grouping of glittering, fresh, lily-like blooms.

Jess kept complimenting Rachel's bunch as if she would far rather Rachel won the right to keep the flowers. In the end, she nodded graciously to Alice, took the other flowers into her own bunch, and led them back through the woods. Rachel was smiling; Alice was beaming with pleasure; Robert was moodily wondering whether he had done wrong; the Queen's face was imponderable.

The ride back was uneventful. Jess was soon in high spirits again, and taught them silly songs to take their minds off their sore backsides and aching legs. 'You'll feel worse tomorrow!' she laughed. 'But the day after we will ride again and you will find it a joy....' Her voice trailed off as her gaze followed an object which cut through the air, a speck almost beyond the sight of the three. She smiled to herself.

9

Homecoming?

They came to the yard by the stables and halted. The Queen handed round apples from a saddlebag and turned to go; then she turned again to Robert and put something into his right hand. 'Give it to her,' she said. She rode off briskly, leaving the children to dismount and lead their ponies to the gate.

Heck was not there. A moody-looking young woman took the ponies and sent the children away quickly. The girls gathered around Rob. He was holding one of the flowers, looking troubled. They insisted that he tell them what was up; and as they walked to the castle, he explained briefly. But he did not mention Jess' words about becoming king, nor her kiss.

'Anyway,' he exclaimed, 'I don't want to give her the flower—why should I?' He made as if to throw it from him, but somehow didn't manage to let it go. Just then they came to the paddock where the two horses were tethered. Their noses were still bound tight and they stood mournfully against the far fence. At the nearer fence, the choir lady was waiting, and she looked up as they approached.

She crossed to them. An eager brightness was upon her face. 'Where is it?' she demanded. 'Give it to me!' She made a snatch at the bunch which Alice held, but Alice evaded her. Robert went to push the lady away from them, but succeeded only in thrusting the flower he held into her hand. The lady grabbed it, clasped it to her breast, and ran immediately from them. They watched her run into the castle.

'What's that?' Rachel had caught sight of something dark on the battlements. They strained their eyes. 'I think it's that—crow, the Ahab-thing. It was circling the palace as we rode in. I saw it.'

'Look!' Something had happened on the palace roof. The creature was turning and leaping, like a cat hot upon a mouse.

Rachel added, 'It was carrying something in its claws when it came in. I didn't see what.'

Now a small figure seemed to leap from the top of the palace. It was gripping the vines which grew up the high grey walls. The crow rose off the roof-top, veered out and then down at the figure, striking with beak and claws. The figure held to the vine with one hand and hit out weakly with the other. The children could not bear to watch, but could not look away. They stumbled back against the paddock and crouched behind the empty black feeding tubs fixed onto the fence there.

Somehow, swaying and slipping on the wall, the figure kept out of the reach of the cruel head and talons of the crow. Reaching a window, it managed to swing itself inside. Ahab forced its neck inside the window, and pulled back suddenly. A scrap of clothes or fur was in its beak. The creature tossed its head back and swallowed what it held. Returning to the window, it beat its wings violently as if to push itself into the room. Finally it backed off and, screeching loudly, flew back to the battlements.

'I hope that person got away.' Rachel spoke what the others were thinking.

Alice startled them. 'It was a hedge-man, a—a Muesli,' she said with certainty. They did not believe her, but it seemed far too likely.

'Down!' Rachel cried suddenly in a low voice. Someone else was now on the battlements. They knew immediately who it was, because Ahab could be seen to bow low before her. She came to the edge of the wall and looked down. She seemed to be asking questions, pointing to the wall and, they supposed, the window which had been used. Then she appeared to be looking towards the stables. They felt her glance fall near them, almost as if it were a ray of hot sunlight on the ground by the paddock. The sensation of her gaze grew nearer; it was very close.

Then suddenly, like the coolness of a cloud passing before the sun's face, they felt her hot gaze no more. Looking up (they had been crouching with their faces nearly touching the ground) they saw the two bound horses standing between them and the Queen.

Rather, one was standing. The stallion had settled onto the ground, and the mare stood just this side of him so that they formed a wall before the children. As the three looked, the mare turned her head to them and made the same hoarse sounds as before. For a few moments they stayed like this, until the stallion gave a 'humph!' and the mare hobbled aside.

They stood. No one was to be seen on the palace walls. With many a backward glance to the suffering animals in the foul paddock, the children ran to the palace and up the stairs to their room.

They found the door open, and much noise coming from within. When they entered, several of the palace guards were opening cupboards, moving beds and searching through chests. The three sat and watched them gloomily. At last the guards left. The door was closed; a key was turned. It was several moments before the meaning of this came to them: they were locked in! Banging on the door returned no response; nor did shouting. Reluctantly they gave it up and began to change clothes.

'I could do with a bath.' Rachel stood, half-dressed, with a towel in her hand.

'I need to use the loo!' Robert replied.

'Don't say that—now you've made me want to go, too.'

'And me. Rachel—where shall I put my flowers?'

'Wrap them in something—where's your handkerchief?'

Alice looked about her, puzzled. 'I dropped it somewhere—I remember that much. It must have been in here. No! It was on the stairs, near the bottom. That Snarl thing was chasing me. I dropped it and almost stopped to pick it up. But I was scared. Then—but—but that was a dream. I was forgetting. It must be in here somewhere.'

'What's wrong, Rachel?' She was staring into space, biting her lip. She was suddenly very pale. Then she reached into the pocket of her dress and slowly pulled Alice's handkerchief from it, showing first a broad blue edge, then bright red elephants.

'Was this it?'

Alice nodded and reached for it. Rachel gave it to her, and said in a dreamy voice, 'I found it on the stairs this morning. Near the bottom.'

They sat a while in silence. Alice's little face was hot and red, and she was twisting her blonde locks about her fingers. She had preferred to believe it was a dream. What if all her dreams turned out to be true? There was the one she used to have—she shivered. Rob took her hand and told her it would be all right. She shook her head.

'Right. Let's discuss. Who's first?' Rachel was taking command again.

'Assume Ali's dream was right.'

'Assume the Queen was there then, and that she sent that Snarl thing to capture us.'

'And what about Ahab? He's horrid and he's her pet.'

'And those poor horses.'

'And I'm sure what Ahab had was a Musey creature.'

'Museling.'

'All right.'

'Shall I throw away the flowers? They must be horrid, too.'

'I don't think they are. If they were horrid she wouldn't guard them,' Robert asserted. But then he fell silent. Jess had been very strange about the flowers.

'Wonder what the choir lady will do with the flower you gave her.'

'Probably eat it.'

'If she breathes on it first, it'll wilt.'

'If she even looks at it, it'll wilt!'

As it happened they did nothing about the flowers because the door was now opened. Lord Lrans stood in the doorway. Rachel threw the towel around herself as he entered.

He spoke politely. 'Evening, ladies...sir. I am sent by Her Majesty to request your presence at a dinner and dance tonight. If you accept it, I will accompany you myself.'

Although he spoke to them, it was obvious that his attention was elsewhere. His eyes were painting the room (so to speak), and his nose kept quivering as though he were sniffing the air. His gaze fell on Alice's flowers, but he did not seem to be at all interested in them. He walked to the window and looked out. Then he closed the window and fastened it securely.

'Please, sir—may we go and wash first?'

'Pardon? Oh, wash—of course you may. Dinner will be in half an hour. The dance will be an hour later, and you may stay or go to bed as you choose.'

He gave a last little sniff, shook his head and muttered something, then strode from the room after politely excusing himself. When his footsteps had died into quietness, they laughed—all three.

'What a fish-cake!' Alice said.

10

The Museling

The dance was unbelievably boring. There were grown-up people and creatures talking about things of no importance at all, dressed in clothes which were uncomfortable and unsightly, eating and drinking things which evidently disagreed with them (you could tell this because their faces became red; their voices became loud and ragged; and their conversation became even more boring).

Most boring of all was the fact that the three longed for their beds but could not go until they had attended enough of the dance to appear polite. Their bodies ached, their eyes were heavy and their hearts were dull.

No doubt the adults believed they were having a wonderful time. Jess, clothed in black silk, sparkled from guest to guest, laughing loudly. She brought one group after another across the room to see the three, introducing Lords and Ladies, Earls and Dukes. At last the children fell back on a well-used trick to escape. They began to yawn widely and rub their eyes when Jess was showing them to these great people. Finally one of the guests remarked how tired they looked; the children quickly denied it; Jess immediately sent them off to bed.

They giggled as they washed and then sprinted up to the room. Adults were very easy to fool—sometimes.

They said their prayers and climbed into the three heavy beds. Alice began to talk sleepily about the ponies. Rachel shushed her. How she longed to sleep!

But there was to be no sleep yet. Before they could drop off, a noise made them sit up in sudden fear. It was a gentle noise—a tapping, soft and repeated, on the window.

'What's that?'

'I don't know.'

'I don't want to know.'

Alice proved to be the bravest of them. She rolled from her bed and walked over to the window.

'Come back, Ali! No—you don't know what it is!'

But Alice had opened the window before the others could leap up and prevent her. A dark shape, about Rachel's size, fell from the window onto the floor and lay there. Alice knelt by it and held it in her arms.

Rachel flew to the light switch. Robert now sat by Alice, gazing at the creature on the floor. It was a Museling, and it was injured. Its brown fur was torn at the left shoulder, and streaks of blood matted its chest. But at first they could look at nothing but its face. Its eyes were so soft, so kind. And yet, how full of pain they were—like the eyes of the horses in that grim paddock.

It was looking up at them with a wan smile on its lips and in its eyes. Its head was shaped something like a badger's or a beaver's, except that the eyes were larger and the jaw broader. The rest of its body was like a bear's, but thinner. Its arms were stubby but muscular; its legs were shorter than a human's would be.

It raised its right arm unsteadily in greeting. 'At last!' it breathed in a high, soft voice. 'We meet, by the Word itself. Yet not, I fear, for long. "At last" is at the last—for me—yes?'

It tried to raise itself, but could not. It gripped Alice's arm and whispered, falteringly, 'You...must go...woods...do not....' But then it spoke no more. Gently they prodded it, called to it, and even shook it; but it did not reawaken.

At last Robert rose.

'We know what tack to use. Heck showed us.'

'Oh, all right,' said Rachel as she moved to the wardrobe. 'I suppose I agree with you. But we've got to be certain.'

'We can't leave it!' cried Alice.

That was a disturbing thought. What if it were found, alive? That Ahab would surely kill it—or worse, torture it. It was like leaving a mouse for a cat to play with.

'Come on then,' spoke Robert. 'We need warm clothes, waterproofs, a coat—weapons?' They gathered what they had, moving as quietly as they could. Their bodies were very stiff from the day's ride. They did not look forward to a ride through the night.

They placed their extra clothes in three bags. Then Robert snapped his fingers. 'How are we to get out? They'll see us!'

Alice went to the window. 'Jump!'

'Break a leg if we did.'

Rachel grinned and began stripping the beds. 'I've always wanted to do this,' she exclaimed, 'and now's the time to try!'

They knotted sheets. At another time they would have giggled helplessly; it would have seemed so funny to be sitting on bare mattresses at midnight, tying together all the bed-linen. But now they were solemn and serious. They fastened the knotted sheets about a huge, heavy wardrobe and threw one end out the window. There was far too much of it. Then they dropped the three bags as well. Slipping and scrambling down the sheet, they scraped their knuckles badly on the wall. They prayed that no one would hear them.

Rachel was last to go. She knelt by the Museling and tried to rouse it, but could not. Sorrowfully she kissed its forehead and walked to the rope. Alice's flowers were on the window-sill. She tucked them into her belt. Then she stopped. A thought had come to her. She pulled up the sheet again and tied its end about the slumbering creature.

The Museling was as light as Robert—much lighter than herself. Even so, it required a great effort to drag it to the window and place it onto the ledge. Its body kept toppling away from her, or giving sudden jerks of pain as she strove to keep it from falling. Then, passing the sheet about her back, she set her legs against the window-sill and pushed it over the edge. She nearly fell herself as the sheet tightened on her, and she cracked her head against the window-frame.

It came to her that she was doing this all wrongly. She should have recalled Robert up to the room to help. Now he and Alice watched, powerless to aid her, as the Museling swung on the sheet's end, bumping none too gently against the wall. Feeling dizzy, Rachel began to pass the sheet out so that the creature fell in short jerks.

'Are you all right?'

She froze, and her heart pounded. It was someone at the door, rattling the key in the lock.

She heard the knob turn. *Lord, help!* She gave a little cry, let the Museling drop the rest of the way to the ground, and leapt for the door. She tried to make herself breathe normally.

The Queen stood before her. Perhaps it was the dizziness—to Rachel she seemed to sway a little. 'Is all well, little one?'

Rachel gave a little yawn—not just to pretend, but also because she badly needed a deep breath of air. She half gasped, 'Yes—yes! Just opening the window. I'll close it now.' (She yawned twice.)

'G'night, Jess.' She closed the door before Jess could respond and leaned against it, listening. The Queen walked away heavily. Or did she? It was so hard to tell. She opened the door again. No one was there. Then she had another idea. The key was in the latch outside. She took it and locked the door from within. It made a terribly loud clonk as it turned. She left the key in the door; that would make it harder for them to open with another key.

Running to the window, she leaned out. Robert gave her a thumbs-up sign. They were huddled together in the shrubbery by the palace wall. Rachel smiled. She had saved the best idea till last. Now she untied the sheet from the large wardrobe and instead passed it around the wardrobe once only. She pulled the end to the window-sill; it came slowly enough, though roughly. Then she jumped off. The free end of the sheet rose from the ground as she descended. Ouch! She hit the shrubbery faster than she wanted to.

Alice and Robert had now guessed the trick. While Rachel picked blackberry thorns out of a bleeding arm, they pulled the sheet until it all passed round the wardrobe and fell to the ground. They shoved most of it behind the shrubs. Now no one would see a sheet hanging from a window and raise the alarm while they were still in the palace grounds. They rolled the Museling onto one sheet and carried it that way, slung between the older two. Slowly, with many a stop, they crept around the castle.

II

Two and One

Bent under the awkwardness of their burden, they hurried through the dark, clouded night towards the stables. It seemed to them that their movements must be heard from within the house: the crunching of gravel, the hollow thumps on the grassy lawns and the swishing against hedges were loud in their ears. Robert was fighting a wish to cough. It hurt him more than any whip could, and he had to keep swallowing hard as the tickle rose in his throat again and again.

At last they came to the small paddock where the two horses stood, attached to one another by rope hobbles which joined their four back legs. Without a word, Rachel climbed over the gate and Robert ran to the door of the stables. While she untied the horses and released their muzzles, he was on his chest feeling for the key under the door.

Now he had it and was turning the key in the lock when Rachel came running to him with a bucket in her hand. He took it and filled it from the tap at his elbow as Rachel pushed open the door of the stables and ran for the tack room. When he had carried the water to the paddock and set it inside the fence, he heard her coming back. She rattled each step because the metal parts of the tack clattered one against the other.

All this time Alice had sat by the Museling's head, alternately peering at its face through the soft darkness and watching the two horses. They limped over to the fence for the water, and the stallion stood back while his mare drank first. Rachel came running then with another bucket, and the two creatures both drank for some time, finishing several bucketfuls each. Between great gulpings, they nuzzled at the children and made strange, thick sounds which they did not understand.

Rachel was pulling at the paddock gate, which was chained but not locked. It squealed rustily as it swung back into the paddock. She shuddered. Someone might hear that. Then she tried to lead the horses out. They were cramped and bruised, and moved no faster than a duck waddles.

'We'll never get far on them!' Rob whispered.

'Not with two of us on each,' she admitted unhappily.

It was a terrible moment. They had imagined that if they could free the horses, they might ride them at a trot out into the fields, back to the place where they had entered the country. But it was now evident that the broken creatures could not carry them far. They must be set free—but they would be of little aid to the children's flight.

'Get them some food!' Rachel hissed. She ran back to the stables, throwing the tack onto the ground. While Rob searched for oats and new buckets, she was pulling ponies out of stalls and hastily putting saddles and bridles on them. Her heart was pounding. Every second brought them nearer capture. Several times she paused, thinking she heard cries from the house, and she ached with weariness and fear. At last she was able to lead four ponies out to the paddock. The horses had eaten and had stumbled over to the gate which opened to the fields behind the stables. Alice had fallen asleep, stretched out on the sheet next to the Museling.

Robert was looking moodily through the gate. 'It's locked,' he muttered as she came up. 'And the moon is about to come out.'

She turned her head away; she didn't want him to see the tears of frustration which ran down her cheeks. They would have to go round by the house now, and out of the front gates—if they were open. All else seemed to be stone walls. She kicked at the gates. They were trapped. And now the moon did leave the thinning clouds to blaze in the sky.

A soft muzzle pushed her to one side. The stallion had come behind her, and now he limped to the gate, turning his head so as to crowd his chest against it. Gathering his hind legs under him, he leaned into the hard iron and then heaved. A tearing, groaning sound of twisting metal broke the night, and then the gates crashed loudly to the earth. The stallion fell upon them, and rolled heavily to his left. Then he rose slowly, panting. His chest gleamed in the moonlight and showed a dark trickle of blood. He snorted to the mare, and the pair limped together along the path. The three children mounted the ponies as swiftly as they could, and followed.

At first they believed that they were undetected. For nearly an hour they crept along the grassy track which they had followed the previous day, stopping now and then for the two horses to nibble grass and regain their wind. Then they came to a crossroads. Ahead lay hills; right and left were woods falling away to distant valleys which gleamed silver beneath the moon and misted stars. With a shake of his head, the stallion led them to the right. He and the mare were moving a little more swiftly now, and Rachel had begun to hope that they would be safe. Her heart kept beating roughly, though, and every small sound made her turn sharply in her saddle.

She looked across to her left at the others; they were nodding, half asleep on the quiet ponies. The Museling rocked from side to side on the saddle where she had tied it with the sheet. Its head rested on the pony's neck, and its arms dangled either side.

As they neared the wood, there came a sound which she knew at once she had been fearing and expecting: a horn blown, like an English hunting horn sounding as the fox is sighted and the final chase to death is begun. The younger children sat upright suddenly in their saddles, and clasped wildly at their reins as the ponies bolted for the trees. Even the two horses were jolted into action, and they began a jerky, pained trot.

Just within the wood there was a shallow stream. The stallion turned into this and walked along it to the left for a hundred yards, then turned right out of the water and plunged into the wood. The others paused. So thick were the branches overhead that the stallion had disappeared into darkness after a few paces; none could tell what lay ahead. Then the horn resounded and they followed doubtfully.

A black hour followed. By hearing and smell they managed to keep in contact with one another as they twisted along unseen paths. At times they strode through thick brush; then they would clomp along hard earth and hear the rattle of small stones knocked by the hooves of their ponies.

Their trail seemed to go roughly parallel to a larger path, from which came from time to time the noise of heavy riding and the shouts of those who searched. Once or twice, far away, there was the baying of hounds. Then came a moment when it seemed certain that they would be discovered.

They had come almost to the main path again, as they knew from the sudden increase in noise and light. The moon still rode in the sky beyond the thick overgrowth of the trees, and it now filtered down on them as they paused. Someone was riding stealthily along the path. They kept as still as they could, and felt their ponies trembling beneath them. A sniffing noise could be heard.

'Who's there?' a harsh voice cried. There was an explosion of movement and a cry; then the sound of thudding hooves; then a great splashing and a cursing. All three smiled as they imagined Lord Lrans sitting in a muddy ditch. But at that moment their mounts bolted, and they had to cling grimly to their saddles to avoid falling as well.

After this, everything became confused. The sounds of the chase grew dim, then suddenly loud; and at last the noises faded and the trek assumed a dream-like quality as they nodded to the hypnotic sounds of monotonous hoof-beats on steadily rising sandy paths. They splashed through dark streams and pushed drowsily among branches prickling with pine needles. Then there came a moment when they were aware that their guides were stopping. The hoofbeats of the stallion, and then of the mare, made a hard, hollow sound for a few paces before ceasing altogether. They could tell by the echoes and the sudden warmth that they were in a cave or passage.

They slipped off their ponies.

'Oh—that does hurt!' whispered Robert drily. 'Move over, Alice. Let me come in a little further.'

'Rob—are we safe now? I'm so tired, I couldn't go on much longer.'

'Where are we, anyway? Come on, Rachel. Bring Doc here next to Grumpy. There's a pool of water he can drink from.'

'Rachel?' The echoes came back to them in a hollow mumble.

Robert went over to her pony. Yet it was not Doc he found, but Happy, with the Museling still tied in the sheet on his back. He felt around the cave and located two horses, three ponies, two children and the Museling. He went to the entrance and called her name. He felt his way to the trees and listened. There was nothing.

He went back to the cave entrance and sat bitterly in the doorway, staring unseeing at the few stars not yet covered by the sudden cold mist.

Rachel was gone.

12

Alone

After a time, exhaustion overcame their anxiety, and they slept. They had taken the Museling from the pony and used the sheet Rachel had wound it in as a ground-cover for the three of them. The ponies stood near the cave's entrance, next to a pile of saddles and bridles. The two horses drank and slept, woke and drank again and then slept where they stood.

When dawn began to transform the sky, Robert woke and, shivering a little, half-walked and half-crawled to the mouth of the cave. His ears might be bad, but in his head he had heard something moving outside. Aching all over and with a throbbing headache, he lay on the cold rock and slowly looked left and right over the dark woods outside the cave. Since the cave was on a hillock, he was looking downwards at the trees. The cave entrance was half hidden by a gorse bush, and he decided to climb out to get a better view of the woods. He carefully wriggled to the left and then upwards, climbing onto a small outcrop of rock which continued for many yards. At the end of this were several leafy shrubs from which he could observe the brightening scene.

Robert lay outside the cave thinking about Alice, who was safely inside it, and Rachel, who was lost somewhere. Then, just as the sun emerged fully from the horizon, he saw a movement on the right side of the woods. At first, he

saw only a series of dark and light flashes between the trees;
then suddenly the moving shapes became two people.

The first was Lrans, not looking as graceful as he had the
other day. His face was dirty and scratched, with a black
left eye. His clothes were muddy and torn. He was talking
earnestly to the Queen, who looked tired and grim. They
came quickly out into the little clearing. Robert was petri-
fied by fear and horror. Should he warn the others? Or if he
tried, would he just give them away?

Then, with sudden despair, he saw Lrans pointing directly at the cave. He could not hear the Queen's question to
him, but he could read her lips: 'Are you certain?' she was
asking.

In the cave, Alice woke and shivered. Where was she? A
thin light straggled through the cave mouth and showed up
the rounded bodies of ponies standing between her and the
entrance. She turned to look for Rachel and then remembered—Rachel was gone.

'Rob?'

No one stirred. The Museling lay near her, and the two
horses were still standing, asleep, at the back of the cave.
Robert, too, had disappeared.

She stumbled to the front of the cave and looked out. A
movement before her and to the right, just at the edge of the
wood, caught her attention, and she had to stifle a cry as she
recognised the Queen and Lrans. She fled back inside,
hardly noticing her aching muscles.

She lay still for a moment, listening to her heart pounding and hearing also the slow, deliberate footsteps of someone approaching the cave. Alice began to gather small rocks
from the sandy floor. If that Queen came in, she would
bombard her. But the footsteps stopped as the Queen's
head came into view, and then they sounded the same slow
pace, this time in retreat. The ponies snorted and dashed
for the back of the cave, and now they were all awake except
the Museling.

From the bushes, Robert had watched the Queen

advance until she could see into the cave: somewhere in the darkness she must have thought she could make out the shapes of horses, ponies and children. She turned about and retraced her steps to the edge of the wood.

She turned back to face the cave and raised her hand. Her voice came like a trumpet across the clearing.

'All crimes can be excused except for treachery. Receive your punishment!'

Her hand fell, and a sea of rocky earth washed down the slope, covering the mouth of the cave. Alice and the horses were trapped inside.

Robert bowed his head to the ground and wept blindly. He tried to rise, but instead he half-fainted and lay helpless with his face pressed into the sand.

After about a minute he became conscious again. He raised his head, expecting to see the two figures bearing down on him; but they were walking back into the woods. To his aching mind there came, again and again, a choice: should he stay here, or should he follow the Queen and...and he didn't know what would happen then.

He ran first to where the cave had been. He put his ear to the heavy earth, but could hear nothing at all. He pounded on the ground and dug at it with his hands, tearing his nails and skinning his knuckles. Still there was no sound, as though the cave had been covered and filled by the landslide. Suddenly, he knew what he must do.

He stood, wiped his eyes, and shook his fist at the woods. He rarely swore, but now the words came tumbling out, ugly and furious. Finally he muttered, 'Just wait until I catch you!'

He set off at a run through the woods. The first strides hurt him badly. The pain made his head clearer, and he concentrated upon fighting his way along the small tangled paths while keeping his sense of direction clear. Brambles tore at his hands and feet. There was no sign of his quarry. His sides ached and he had to stop several times to recover his breath.

Then he came out onto a larger track. At the far end, a white and a dark shape were moving off the track to the left. They were perhaps a quarter of a mile away. He felt strength flood into his chest and ran faster than before. A few minutes later, he too turned off into a small copse. He ran until he fell with exhaustion at the far edge of it.

He could see the Queen, not forty yards away, mounting her white stallion at the side of the main road along which they had ridden last night. He opened his mouth to shout a challenge to her. But just then a furry paw slipped across his face. Strong arms pinned him against the ground. A voice whispered to him words he could not understand because they were so soft, and directed at his bad ear.

13

The Tide Begins to Turn

Robert was too angry to be afraid. Hot, sharp words came to his mind and desperate actions sprang into his imagination. He was about to bite—hard—at the animal-smelling paw which was clamped over his mouth when it was suddenly removed. A weight rolled off his back, and he heard a soft voice call: 'Turn round then, creature. Let us have a look at you.'

Robert looked up. The horses were specks on the road, speeding back to the palace. He sat up with a hopeless hostility in his heart and glared at the Museling who was watching him. 'Why didn't you let me chase after them?' he shouted at the animal.

The Museling was sitting on the ground, leaning against a tree trunk. Its fur was a blotchy grey like the tree's bark; its eyes were like two dark acorns. If Robert had not been looking for it, he would easily have missed seeing it among the shifting shadows. Now it reached forwards and plucked a few strands of rough grass which it began to chew thoughtfully. After a few moments it answered in a small voice: 'You were brave to try. But it would have meant death.'

'I suppose you're right,' Robert admitted reluctantly. 'Not that it matters.'

The creature studied his face. 'Can you mean that? Is your life such a small thing that you can throw it aside like this?' It flipped a blade of grass to the ground.

'She killed my friends.'

'And so? You let her take you as well? Listen, my furless beast—she has killed or maimed many of my family. But I do not run to her in open daylight and beg her to finish me off too. Slowly, slowly, we grind away at her power and very soon she will fall. That is, she will fall unless you lose your head and give her the chance to escape again.'

'What d'you mean? What's it all to do with me? Why do you blame me? That's hardly bloomin' fair!'

The creature turned its head from side to side. 'I do not know what you mean, white-skinned wonder. But if you can think, you can see that what matters is the doing of what we should do. You can help overthrow the Queen. Or you can help keep her in power. Which do you choose?'

'To get rid of her, of course. She killed my—'

'You think she has done this thing. She thinks she has done this thing. Thinking is not the same as doing!'

'I saw it. There was this cave, you see. And they were inside—at least Alice was—and *she* came up with that Lumbago or whatever he's called. And then—'

He stopped because the creature was laughing—quietly at first, then with a good throaty chuckle. 'You must excuse me, pale man. I was thinking how shocking it will be for her when she sees you next. She will think that her spells have worked backwards or that she is going mad—ah! what a pleasure to see the look on her face then!'

The Museling stopped and looked earnestly at the boy. 'You think I am making cruel fun of you. You must decide what to believe—your eyes or your heart. Even were your friends dead, they would rise again when the worlds are changed. But it has not come to that! One I saw in the woods before morning broke; another I can tell you will soon be laughing in the Chamber of Meeting far below us. With her is a red-furred rascal called Phiana whom you rescued. She is almost awake. For which,' he arose and bowed, 'I owe you thanks. She is my sister.' He held out his paw, palm upwards. 'Dannos—your friend.'

Robert put his hand lightly on the other's paw, suddenly

uncertain how one shook hands in this place. 'Robert,' he said shyly.

The creature slid his paw away after a few moments. The surface of the paw was like the rough, fur-surrounded underside of a cat's paw, but wider. The fingers—if you could call them that—were very short and were topped by hard, curving nails.

'Now, friend Robert,' (he pronounced it 'Wobbit'), 'we have a fair journey before us. By nightfall, we must have followed the wood around until we are as near the city as we might come. Then we must enter and cause a small disruption. Perhaps we will even free a few of my people who lie in her dungeons.' He nodded towards the road the Queen had followed. He stamped angrily upon the ground and shook his clenched paw towards her. Robert stared at him in wonder, and then nodded his head in agreement.

'Friend Dammos—' ('Dannos!' the other cried) 'Dannos—yes, I'll come. But I don't think I'll go very fast. I feel like a spider that's had its legs pulled off.'

Dannos looked at him worriedly. He counted the boy's legs.

'You have only two. Were there more?'

Robert laughed, and then they both laughed. Dannos pulled the furless boy to his feet and they set out to their left along the edge of the forest, keeping just within the shade of the trees as the sun rose in the clear sky.

The sun had become high and hot when Dannos turned and saw that Robert could go no further for a while. He had been bravely forcing himself to match the brisk pace of the Museling, and for the first hour had been sure of his ability to keep up. But then tiredness and pain had crept from his joints and converged on his head. Strange noises were sounding in his ears. Black spots were beginning to slide across his vision as he pushed aside what must have been the thousandth bramble and saw the Museling looking back at him with worry.

'Is it well?' They had hardly spoken up to now, so intent

was the Museling on making a morning's progress through the wood.

'I can manage,' Robert muttered grimly. He wiped his face. 'Is there any water nearby?'

Dannos came close up to him and looked at his face. 'I know so little about your sort of animal,' he said. 'Tell me, when one of your kind changes colour, is it a sign that you are, say, unwell? Or do all of you become a gentle shade of green after a morning's walk?'

For answer Robert sat down. 'To be honest, Danny, I feel sick. And my tongue is like a dried-up sponge.'

'Let me see...no, surely not. A sponge has small holes throughout and its surface is most uneven. Your tongue, now—oh, *I* see. You mean that you are thirsty!'

Suddenly serious (Robert looked like keeling over at any moment) the little creature pulled the boy up and half-carried him to the shade of a tree. Then from a bag slung over his left shoulder he produced a small flask.

'Here, drink this.... My, you have drunk it all in one gulp!'

'Is there more?'

'Do you always drink so much?'

'That's only a little drink for me.'

The creature's eyebrows (rather, where his eyebrows would have been if he had not been quite covered in fur) shot up, and he sat back a few moments thinking about this. Then, with a quick explanation that he would look for a stream, he shot off into the deep woods. Robert listened intently to the gentle sounds of his departure, then heard the birdsong high in the trees, and while he followed the notes across the sky, he fell into a blessed sleep.

It seemed hours before he was shaken softly. In reality, he had slept only twenty minutes. Dannos had the flask in his hand, newly filled.

After emptying it again, Robert felt refreshed enough to rise and follow Dannos into the wood to the stream he had found. There he drank greedily and noisily while the creature watched him with amazement.

'Boy wonder,' it called to him from its position crouching on the bank above him, 'if you wish to wash, or relieve yourself, or sleep—this is a safe area. I will be gone for some time seeking food and news. Can you wait until I return?'

Robert nodded, wiping his mouth on his sleeve. He would like to do all three. But as Dannos sped away, he decided that he most of all wanted to sit by the stream and dabble his sore feet in it. He fumbled to untie his laces and with a sigh dropped his bare feet into the coolness of the clear water.

It was pleasant to be able to do all this—to be able to drink from a stream, to watch it sparkle cleanly in the sunlight, to splash about in it. In Overton you could not drink the water. In most of the world, you could not safely drink the water of a stream. And if you were to try and walk in a stream, you had better wear something on your feet because of the tins and broken glass. You had to ask yourself, 'Is it polluted? What factories are nearby? Is there a nuclear power plant? Where is the sewage works?' The world must surely be a filthy place. Why?

He had reached no conclusion within the next half-hour, so he dried his feet and had a brief wash. When Dannos found him again, he was sleeping once more, this time curled up on some leaves he had raked together beneath an old willow. He sat up immediately as the Museling came close.

He had been dreading the 'food', expecting moist, smelly fungi and bitter rose hips. Dannos had, however, brought bread and a small bottle of wine, followed by some nuts like pecans. Bread without butter is dry, but it went down very well. Again, Dannos was surprised to see how much he drank, and now ate.

'Are you sure you need all this?' he kept asking. 'Truly you are of the same race then as the woman—you know the one I mean. They say she eats and drinks enough for a week at every meal. And the banquets—this last week over a quart of wine per person: and not watered wine, as this is.'

'You seem to know a lot about what happens at the palace.'

'I do know! We have some who oppose the Queen, but are made to work for her. That is fair, you know. You can do your work as a maid or a stableman even though you do not love the one who pays you.'

'A stableman? Like—you mean, Heck?'

The creature nodded. 'He was her stableman, and an honest one. No horse went untended.'

'You said "was". Is Heck all right? He helped us, you know.'

'I did not know. And no, he is not "all right". He is in prison, awaiting what the Queen calls justice. And we know what that means.'

'No, I don't. What does it mean?'

'He tried to feed two creatures the Queen had ordered to be starved. They took him yesterday evening to the dungeons. Today they will leave him to think of tomorrow. Tomorrow he will be killed.'

Robert had risen to his feet, brushing the crumbs from his lap. Thoughts of the Queen had come unpleasantly and suddenly into his mind. He had lain face down outside the cave while she had tried to destroy those inside. Well, he wasn't going to lie down this time.

'Where are you going?'

'With you of course.'

'Without knowing where I go?'

Robert nodded. Dannos smiled and held out his paw again. Robert slapped his hand down on it firmly this time, and the other grinned at him with great pleasure.

'Boy wonder indeed! Come then, hairless beast!'

'Lead on, then, fuzzy-face!' Robert immediately replied, and was rewarded by seeing those non-existent eyebrows shoot up again. The Museling chuckled and they set off.

14

Dangerous Dan

This time there was not far to travel. Dannos had arranged shelter for them at a safe house in the city, and they needed only to reach the wood's edge a few miles distant where horses would be waiting.

As they walked, Robert told of their arrival and their escape. The Museling tried to explain a little of his own history, but it was difficult to follow because there turned out to be at least four Museling groups, known by the colour of their fur, and Dannos' mother was a Black whereas his father had been a Red. Dannos was (confusingly) a Grey, and had gone off at the age of twenty to live with the Greys. He was now one hundred and thirty-seven, and was one of the youngest of his clan.

'But how does a Black mother and a Red father make you a Grey?'

Dannos shrugged. 'You may as well ask where the Queen came from.'

'All right, then, where did she come from?'

'One hundred and thirty-three years ago, she arrived from somewhere in this universe, bringing with her a number of her own race. If I knew where she came from, I would send to ask them to take her back!'

'One hundred and thirty-seven is awfully old to be the youngest of your clan.'

'Since she came, there have been no births among us. Even among her own race there have been no births. This at least means that she can do little yet, because her army and her city cannot grow. Yet she somehow brings in new people, a few at a time, like sand which drops grain by grain through a pin-hole in a bag.'

'What about Ahab?'

'He was her husband. By some means, he was transformed into that hideous creature.'

'She did that to her husband?'

'Hush!' They had reached the edge of the wood. The Museling was concentrating hard, as if listening to something. Robert, too, tried to listen, but heard only an odd far-off babble in his head. Then, nearer at hand, he thought he heard a soft 'come!' He stepped forward at the same moment as Dannos.

A Red Museling was there, a full foot shorter than Dannos and much rounder. He nodded to them both and glanced nervously about.

'I brought the ponies. Couldn't get 'orses. She's commandeered the lot for a big parade. Wants to make a spectacle of 'erself agin, wrapped up in a new pretty fur from some poor creature what should be wearin' it itself.... Pleased to meet you, um, Wobbit. My name's Casca, if Dannos the Dangerous here 'asn't told you. Don't s'pose he 'as, though, cos he's allus too busy planning things like breakouts and breakins and riots and demonstrations against your friend and mine, Ruby Red-lips at the palace. Never 'as time to think of anything else, 'as poor Dannos.'

After this long introduction, Robert couldn't think of anything to say except 'hello', and to hold out his hand in true Museling fashion, which seemed to please the little Casca no end. He chuckled and slapped the extended hand with a mighty smile on his face and then beamed at Robert as if he were the King of England, and not the noisiest boy in The Elizabeth Mayhem Memorial Orphanage and the most reluctant scholar ever to hit Overton Primary.

Dannos clapped Casca on the back and called him a clown, which Casca seemed to like, and they put their heads together for a few moments and talked quietly while Robert studied them both.

'Wobbit—we'll need to wait here until dark. Casca says that crow is about. He's brought more food.'

'An' lots of drink. Deadly Dan was particular about bringing lots to drink. Says you nearly emptied Flashpond stream. So I brought wine, raspberry cordial and water. Buckets of the stuff!'

They retired to the shade of a large beech tree to wait the few hours until dark. As they ate and drank, the two Muselings shared with Robert the plans for that night and for the early hours of the coming morning.

'Tonight is the best time, see?' said Dannos, carefully brushing crumbs from his dark fur. 'It will be misty, for a start.'

'An' there's gonna be a fair eclipse near midnight,' finished Casca.

Rob nodded slowly. He was trying hard to understand. 'What's this...this fairy clips. What's it like?' he asked.

'Dark an' eerie,' replied Casca, 'an' about half an hour long.'

Robert nodded again, as if he had half an idea of what they were talking about. He tried to imagine a small, blackened winged creature, mysterious and short-lived, and armed with...with clips? It was going to be an unusual night.

15

The Diversion

Darkness was slow in coming. To pass the time, they talked of their lives and especially their childhoods. Dannos described with mirth the pranks of Casca—how he had once dyed his legs yellow so as to be let off school with 'an unknown disease'; how he had crept inside the palace of the Queen when she was newly arrived and heard her plans; how he had recently taken the keys to the palace and hung them on a hook some fifteen feet above the door so that the guards had to fetch ladders and retrieve them.

They were fascinated to hear Robert's account of his years in various homes: the different matrons and masters who had sometimes beaten their children, sometimes coddled them; the food, which could be disgusting and cold, or delicious and plentiful if you had a good cook at the home; the other children, who were for the most part cheerful despite their hard lives. 'The Black Hole' at Overton wasn't all that bad. There were chips and eggs and sausages and spaghetti and Sunday roast and plenty of home-made cakes and biscuits—and the houseparents were kind.

'And your real parents?'

'They don't tell you about them. Think they're afraid we'd be running off to find them. But not me! If they didn't care enough to keep me, I'm not likely to go looking them up.'

'P'raps there was some reason—p'raps they was ill or something,' suggested Casca.

Robert just shook his head and stared towards the city. They sat in silence for a time, before the Muselings rose and resaddled the ponies. The cloudy sky had gone grey, then reddened at one edge and finally blackened. There were no street lights, and darkness was precisely that: *dark*. Robert found that he liked it; perhaps those street lights which stole the darkness from the town of Overton were just another kind of pollution, like the waste from the factories which stole the freshness from the river.

The four miles to the city went quickly, and soon they were in a small house. A short, lean, smiling old woman with a wrinkled face and frizzy white hair bustled in and out of the primitive kitchen, bringing them cheese and bread, and more wine. After one glass, Robert had to ask for water instead—never had he had so much wine in one day, or one month!

The woman's name was Nancy: she had been a tramp in America. She had slept rough, travelling from place to place by stowing away in railway cars or climbing onto buses when the driver wasn't looking. Then one day she had met a gentleman who had offered her what he called 'a new life'.

' "New," he said! "Your own house, food, a little garden, maybe even a car if things go well." Said it was a new trading venture and gave me some paper to sign. Well—I'd never learned to read, but I could write my name and I had tried most things, long as they were legal and proper. I never done anything indecent, you know? So I says "yes" and here we are.'

'What do you do in the city?'

'Like all the others, I work in one of the factories. I'm a packer. They send down the line a batch of perfumes'—she pronounced it *par-fumes*—'or such-like, and I put them in their boxes and seal them up in the wrappers.'

'You see, Wobbit,' said Dannos, 'the Queen makes things here, and somehow takes them back to your place, to your world.'

The other Museling interrupted, 'At first, she tried sellin' 'em to us. But as Dangerous 'ere will tell you, no Museling

ever bought anything, no, nor sold so much as 'alf an acorn!
So she gives that up, see, after puttin' a few in prison and
murdering some others. No creature would work for her,
either; she 'ad to bring 'em all in from elsewheres.'

'And as Casca would say if he had as much tact as even a
dandelion has, some of those the Queen brought have been
good friends rather than otherwise. Like Nancy here, and
Heck, and many more.'

Nancy laughed cheerfully. 'Some friends! What quality
you fellows get to mix with! An old tramp here, a former
prisoner there, here a drunk, there a skunk, everywhere an
old punk!'

'And all of 'em God's children, if they wants it,' put in
Casca mildly. 'And if so, then in my family.' He held out his
hand to Nancy, who grinned and slapped it playfully.

'And what of tonight, then, boys? What's the game?'
Nancy glanced about to see that the clean but threadbare
curtains were drawn fully across the windows. They told
their plans in quiet voices, punctuated by roars of her
laughter. At the end, tears of mirth were running down her
face.

'If that doesn't beat the lot! Well, well. But surely, it's a
bit risky—for the boy, that is.'

'The first part, perhaps. But once we are inside...'

'Wait!' She sat with one hand raised, the other on her
head to show that she was thinking hard. 'What about this
for an idea?'

Shortly after midnight, just as the light of the moon was
being wiped from the sky by the promised eclipse, a small
cloaked figure was seen rattling the front gate of the palace.
When the guard approached, he saw an old woman who
worked in Factory 7.

'Go home!' he bullied. 'No one is allowed in once the gate
is closed for the night.'

She argued, but he shouted back, 'If you have problems
at home, see the street police officer!'

'But I was told to come here at once. The Queen will

want to hear what I have to say. She won't forgive you if you don't at least take a message to her. And why shouldn't you let me in? You're not afraid of a poor, frail old lady like me, now are you?'

She whispered something through the bars, at which the burly guard stiffened. Then he ran into the palace. A few moments later he returned and cautiously unlocked the gate, looking carefully about him as he did so. The woman entered, and he locked the gate behind her. He did not notice that the deepening shadows by the wall had been joined by three others. Taking advantage of his absence from the gate for less than a minute, two dark creatures and one light one with his face blackened by soot had climbed onto the sturdy shoulders of the 'poor, frail old lady' and from there had pulled themselves onto the wall and over into the cool darkness.

16

Trick or Treat

Nancy was let into the palace by the butler who took her through to a large room downstairs—the Queen's office. The Queen herself was seated at a broad wooden desk reading some papers. She did not look up until the old woman stood before her; then she nodded to the butler who left quietly, shutting the door behind him.

'Now, Miss Preston, what is all this about a plot?'

Nancy curtseyed before speaking, and kept her gaze on the desk as though too shy to look the Queen in the face. (In fact, she was using the little reading ability she had to scan the papers which the Queen had carelessly pushed towards her.)

'It's like this, Your Majesty. I was out walking in the dark, just after curfew—sorry, Ma'am, I was just longin' for some fresh air, I won't do it again—and I stopped by Mere Field for a spell. Some creatures came up and I heered them talkin'. They spoke of something happenin' tonight. Didn't hear it all, but they said something about "striking first" and "factory 22". But that can't be right, Ma'am, cos there's only twenty-one factories.'

She stole a glance at the Queen's face. It had gone white. Nancy hid a smile. She had told the truth—she had gone to Mere Field, and the others had said just what she had repeated, so that she could tell it to the Queen. And the Muselings knew about a secret factory '22'—which was a building outside the city, set into the side of a hill. Few in the city knew about it. Not even the Muselings knew what it was for.

'Look at me.' At the Queen's command, Nancy raised her eyes demurely to her face.

'Swear that you have told me nothing but the truth.'

'I swear it.'

The Queen held the eyes of the woman for a long moment. 'What else was said?'

'Nothing that I heard, Your Majesty—except that they said something about there being a hundred on foot, and some on ponies. Then they moved away.'

The Queen turned to leave the room. Then, as if bitten by a sudden thought, she stopped and jerked around to face Nancy again. Her face took on a look of cunning, but her voice was very sweet as she asked: 'Have you told anyone else about this—this "factory"?'

'No, Your Majesty.'

The Queen smiled and rushed from the room. Within moments, there came sounds of people and creatures running through the palace. Doors slammed, both in the palace and in the buildings within the palace grounds. Soon the stamping and shouting made it clear that many soldiers had assembled by the front gates. The Queen and Lrans held a quick, whispered discussion in the entrance hall, just outside the door to the Queen's office. By moving near to the door, Nancy was able to catch the last part of the conversation.

'...or the other, they will be overstretched. They cannot protect the tunnels and attack 22.' This was the Queen.

'Which do you suggest I deal with first—the tunnels or the force at the factory?'

'What do *you* think?'

'They will be relying upon darkness to cover them—but it will aid us equally well. If we were to come up behind the factory, they would be much surprised. And we would have the wind behind us.'

'And if they noticed, we can therefore attack the way we

both have in mind. And you could collect a good stock of poison to use in the tunnels. Go then.'

Lrans bowed. Grinning broadly, he soon mounted a black horse and rode out through the gate. The soldiers followed him.

There was silence. The whole of the palace seemed to have been emptied, except for a few servants. Nancy had tiptoed back to the desk and was puzzling at the papers. She regretted—for the first time—that she had not tried to learn to read at all until coming to this land. She could make out the sense of very little of the papers. What was all this about 'mustard' and 'nerve'?

Just then the Queen returned. With her was the guard who had been at the gate. She said nothing, but nodded towards the old woman. The guard approached and took Nancy's arm firmly. He pulled her through the door, then out of the palace. When she stumbled, he dragged her. She cried out, and he simply cursed and kicked her.

'Where are you taking me?'

'You know.'

He pulled her upright and forced her to walk before him in what was now nearly complete blackness.

'You're going to the prisons, of course,' he gloated. 'Surely you didn't think Her Majesty would leave you free, and you knowing so much?'

He entered a dark, winding tunnel, and they walked about twenty yards down a steep ramp. Shadows were thrown back at them by a dim lamp ahead. They were now underground, and came to a steel gate. On the other side of this gate two more soldiers sat at a table, playing cards.

'Shiffle!' the guard called. 'Open for one more prisoner, if you will. Her Majesty says you may put her in any cell you wish. Bread and water are to be permitted her. Here is the pass.'

A large, broad soldier rose and came to the gate, wiping his mouth with his hand. He studied the sheet of paper handed to him, read down to the Queen's signature, and grunted. Then he took from his pocket a large key with which he opened the gate.

He stood back as the guard pushed Nancy inside. As the new soldier grasped her arm roughly, the palace guard himself suddenly fell against the gate, as if shoved from behind.

'Hey! Go back!' the soldier began.

The gate swung hard against him and knocked him off balance. At the same time the old lady somehow twisted his plump, well-muscled arm behind his back, hooked her leg through his, and tripped him so that he fell flat upon his face with her knee in his back. He groaned as she grasped his other arm and with surprising strength jerked it around to join the first.

The guard and the other soldier were simultaneously set upon by two small, powerful creatures whose anger burned so hotly that the men fell back before them and were quickly overpowered. A young boy with a blackened face came round to them in turn and tied their hands and legs together. Then they were firmly gagged.

'All *right!*' exclaimed Nancy in an excited whisper, and she slapped the hand of Robert and the paws of the Muselings with gusto. 'Worked like a dream!'

They looked at the three bound soldiers.

'They do not deserve to live, truly...,' began Dannos.

Casca interrupted, 'Never said a truer word, Danny— oughta be dropped in the river wiv a couple of crocodiles to keep 'em company. But I've never hurt even a fly if I could avoid it, and nor you. Leave 'em to stew in their consciences. P'raps they'll 'ave a change of 'eart.'

Dannos nodded reluctantly.

'Come on, boys!' said Nancy, sucking her knuckles where they had been grazed on the rock floor. 'Business first, philosophy after.'

Robert had said nothing since climbing over the palace gates. Remembering his orders, he began to rub the soot off his face, using water from a bowl by the soldiers' guard-room. The others took keys from the guard-room and ran off down the passage. Soon, creatures of all descriptions were walking or crawling or hobbling up the tunnel from the cells where they had been kept for days or years.

One gnarled and grey old Museling limped up, leaning on a man whose hair kept falling in his face. He flicked it back over his ears and smiled at Robert.

'Heck!'

'The same, young master. And much obliged to you for coming to visit. But I'm afraid the Queen's accommodation isn't the most gorgeous of stabling!'

He left the old Museling to lean against the wall while he trotted back to assist some others from their cells.

Soon around one hundred creatures were assembled. They moved through the gates, which Dannos relocked, leaving the soldiers within. He left the key in the lock for the soldiers to use once they had worked free of their bonds.

'Now, Wobbit. Part two of the plan. Are you ready?'

Robert nodded. He and Casca hurried out of the tunnel and around to the back of the palace grounds. They felt their way to the stables through the darkness which had come down like a sea of ink around them. Using the guard's keys, they unlocked the gate—which had been repaired since its destruction the night before—and swung it wide open. Meanwhile, Heck had opened the stables and was saddling all the ponies and horses he could find. As the weaker prisoners were led or carried to him, he set them upon a mount, sometimes with an able-bodied ex-prisoner sitting behind them to hold them on. At last the horses, ponies and creatures were all out of the gate—except for Casca and Robert.

'Part three?' Robert asked, grinning.

'With pleasure, Wobbit. Give 'er a shock, shall we?'

They ran to the palace. It was easy to decide which room the Queen was in—it was the only lighted one on the ground floor. Casca let Robert climb upon his shoulders. They stood outside one of the lighted windows.

'She's in there, but looking down at the desk.'

'Right then, Super Wob, 'ere we go. Tell me when to do

the floating act.' Casca began a series of ghastly hooting moans.

Robert, streaks of soot still upon his face, stared sternly in at the Queen.

She looked up suddenly. There—at the window! A ghostly figure, scowling at her, seemed to float across the panes. It was—no, surely—no, it *was!* Colour left the Queen's cheeks for the second time that evening. The ghost had disappeared, its unearthly moaning had ceased, and she sat rigid, staring at the window.

She was not afraid of ghosts. She had made too many ghosts in her time to fear them, and she had great authority over evil spirits.... But she was disturbed nonetheless. Her massive powers, accumulated over the centuries in many worlds, had been challenged. Never before had a ghost dared to taunt her. This one had stared at her insolently— and then, just before it had passed into the mists of night, it had clearly *stuck out its tongue at her*.

17

Alice in Underland

When the Queen had raised her hand outside the cave and uttered her curse, Alice had been standing with the ponies and horses. There was a shudder then that threw her to the ground. The earth roared; the light went out; the air was choked with dust. She covered her face and, with the others, crowded blindly to the back of the cave, coughing and gasping. Her eyes were stinging from the dirt.

Then it was quiet. Slowly the air cleared. It remained dark, but by touch she located all the creatures except for the Museling. She crawled forward until her hands contacted the sheet, which she pulled back with the creature on it.

'What do we do now?'

There was no answering voice, and now at last she began to cry. The ponies snorted reassuringly, and the mare nuzzled against her, making queer noises, but this was no comfort. They were trapped. They would stay like this for hours, or days, or weeks until they died from lack of air and water. Suddenly she realised that this had been exactly the Queen's intention.

A long time passed, in which she sometimes prayed, sometimes shouted until her voice was hoarse, and sometimes sat and stared unthinking into the dark. She may even have fallen asleep—her mind was so confused and oppressed by the suffocating darkness that she lost track of the minutes.

Then the noises began. At first they were distant rustling and scrabbling sounds, like someone wrapping Christmas presents. Then the sounds became more like an army of rats chewing through a skirting board. Then she realised that they were the sounds of digging—not of digging with tools, but with hands, or paws.

Suddenly Alice was afraid. This must be one more part of the Queen's calculated cruelty. She wanted the captors to begin to hope, and then there would be this horrible moment when what emerged from the earth was more dreadful even than dying slowly in this blackness.

Alice put her hands over her ears and shut out the sound. But she removed them when a new sound was heard—the sound of a musical humming. Whatever was digging was singing while it worked! Just as suddenly as she had been afraid, she was now certain they were safe. She shouted, and from very close indeed a muffled shout answered her.

A few moments later, a light showed along a sandy crack; then a clump of earth fell away near her shoulder and she had to cover her eyes from a sudden brightness. Peering from between her fingers, she saw first a cool, steady white light. Then she saw the great black paw which held the light, and the long muscular arm of a large Museling. Its hair was shining black, and its teeth flashed white under its dark eyes.

Pushing its way through the heavy earth like a man wading through water, it regarded her for a moment, then lowered its light and looked about the cave. When it spoke, its voice was quiet but agitated: 'The others! Where are the others?'

Alice shook her head, for the moment lacking courage to speak. It pointed to the pile of rubble that had spilled in through the entrance.

'Are they in *that?*'

'No. They were outside when it happened. I don't know where.'

The creature nodded. It crossed quickly over to the sleeping Museling and placed its head upon the bloodied chest. For a long minute it listened and stared into the darkness. Then, as if suddenly remembering its manners, it rose and held out its paw to Alice, palm up.

'I am Mara. But...,' it seemed to become embarrassed. 'But perhaps you will use my nickname, like everyone else. They call me Tiny.'

Alice had to reach up to place her hand on top of the Museling's. 'I'm Alice. I don't have a nickname.'

'Then I will call you giant!' laughed the other. 'That way, no one will be confused.'

One of the ponies snorted indignantly, and Mara called out to Alice, 'He says that we may call him anything so long as I get some water to him soon.'

The Museling then carried on a long unintelligible conversation with the horses before turning again to Alice.

'Thank you, giant friend, for taking such care of my dear Phiana.' It nodded to the sleeping Museling. 'Indeed, it was good that you did so, for when I began to dig, it was only because of Phiana that I knew where to dig.'

'You mean she called you, or something like that?'

'Something like that. She may not have called, but I heard. She and I were little Muselings together when the world was much younger; then young wives together; how could I not hear? And I heard around her the sounds of horses, and danger, and terror—and children. Also, I knew they were in a cave near to our tunnels. But come, there is time for explanations later. This place is not safe for long.'

She nodded to the pile of rubble, which was being added to gradually by falls of sand and stone from the roof. Then she turned and spoke into the hole she had come from. Alice realised now that the noises of digging had continued while Mara had been in the cave; looking beyond the tall creature, she saw other Muselings toiling at the hard earth.

It was exciting and awesome to see how the Muselings widened the hole in the hard and rocky soil with sweeps of their rough, broad paws, using them as though they were spades working on some powerful steel digging machine. The dirt was quickly moved from the tunnel and piled against the other rubble until there was a space wide enough for Alice and the ponies to travel along, followed by 'Tiny' carrying Phiana.

They descended rapidly for about ten yards until they came to a wide tunnel. Tiny settled the other Museling here and rushed back to the cave. After a few minutes more of noisy digging, she came down the tunnel again, leading the horses. These seemed to be quite at home here, stamping the floor, looking about, and snorting to one another as if to say, 'Do you remember?' and, 'It's hardly changed at all, has it?': which is in fact exactly what they were saying.

Soon the other Muselings came back into the tunnel, and a hasty conference was held in a language that moved so fast that Alice felt sure no one could understand it even if he could speak it. Then some of the Muselings disappeared back into the cave, apparently to finish off some digging, while another couple went running down the tunnel and one remained with Mara. Between them the two Muselings carried their injured friend. Alice followed with the horses and ponies, feeling it very odd that she should be in such a dark tunnel at around eight o'clock on a summer's morning.

18

The Conference

They hurried along the dim corridors. These were lit at long intervals by the same soft globes as the one Mara carried in her left paw. As they descended, the light grew and there were gentle noises of creatures moving about, muttering and laughing (and how comforting it was for Alice to hear laughter and singing). The ponies and horses turned off into one of the side passages, snorting goodbyes to the Muselings as they went.

'You will see them again soon. They have smelled their way to the stables.'

At last they turned into a long hall which was furnished with a good, solid oak table flanked by benches along its length. Obviously a large group of creatures was accustomed to sitting here over meals. Alice's stomach began to grumble, and she sniffed the air. Fresh bread!

Mara laughed as she caught Alice's glance. She spoke to a companion, who took the injured Museling into yet another room, calling to someone as he entered. Mara then led Alice to the table, and cried in a loud voice, 'Food here! Food for a giant, if you please!'

Unhurried, a furry, wrinkled, reddish face poked itself around a door-frame. Its eyes became very wide, but it said nothing and the face disappeared again. Crockery and cutlery clattered and clonked, followed by the softer sounds of cutting and arranging and preparing of food. Lastly, the red Museling reappeared with a tray.

There was bread, butter and honey. There was creamy milk and something like tea. There was something crunchy and sweet which Alice poured milk over and ate like cereal while the Muselings stared at the performance. Then there was a sweet apple to crunch, the sort of apple which is so juicy that you half-eat, half-drink it. For eating she had one bowl, and a rounded metal object which served as both a spoon and a blunt knife.

She stared about her. The room was a rocky cavern which had been shaped and carved and then polished lovingly until it gleamed in the soft light. Doors had been added—great uneven slabs of wood swinging from brown frames, shining like the walls.

While she ate, the old cook—named Feather—asked her about her home, her world and her brief history in their world. Mara sat and listened. Her eyes were sometimes very distant, as though she were thinking of things happening far away—thoughts of unvisited seas and unreachable stars. But she heard all that was said.

'And you stayed with the great lady herself?' This was Feather, whose voice was low, and soft like his bread. With his paws he made the shape of a crown upon his head to indicate that he was talking of the Queen. 'A beautiful woman on the outside. Like a shiny, poisonous berry.' He pretended to eat such a berry and clutched his throat, making choking sounds.

Alice realised that he was trying to make her feel at ease, and she laughed gratefully. 'She was all right at first. She was awfully kind to us.'

'She was kind to me, too!' He held out his left paw. One of his claws was missing. 'She took away a finger I didn't need! And all I had done was to say I wouldn't make my bread for her to sell!'

'Your bread *is* very nice.' She took a bite. It had the soft, mellow flavour of ordinary wheat bread, but there were other tastes, too: tastes of fruits and nuts—and it had a sweet, gentle fragrance.

'But my baking is a gift from God to me, and my bread is

a gift to others. I sell nothing; I give everything. We do not live here by buying and selling, but by giving. And when you accept my bread, you accept my hand, and we are friends.' He held out his right paw in that peculiar Museling way, and Alice gripped it, her heart warmed by his kindness.

'If only Rachel—and Robert—' she began, but could go no further. She cried miserably, her little shoulders shaking. Feather patted her softly on the back. For a long time there was silence.

'We will find them.' This time Mara spoke, and her voice was firm. 'But the world is moving fast. We have plans to make. Come, we are called.'

Alice looked up. No one was to be seen, but both Mara and Feather were clearing and resetting the table in preparation for something. Within a few minutes several Muselings of all colours and other creatures began to assemble in the hall, and within another few minutes, something like steaming cocoa was brought round to them all. It tasted of hazelnuts and cream.

Sipping her 'cocoa', she studied the new creatures shyly. She did not yet know, but soon guessed that most of them were not natives to this world. They had slipped by accident through those same gaps in the boundaries between worlds which the Queen had used to bring in people for her city. There was a small dragon, a leg-serpent, and a Tove— creatures she had met in books, but had thought to be make-believe. She began to wonder whether all those creatures in stories—gryphons, unicorns and so on—had really existed, and had found their ways to earth through these holes in the universe, like the hole she had entered through.

Before she could think further, a commotion at the main door of the hall took her attention. Something knee-high, round and very active was bouncing about while carrying on a conversation with Mara. It was a very strange discussion, because the creature supplemented its words by twirls in mid-air, or by spinning giddily about. It was not a serious talk, though—Mara was chuckling and the creature was beaming all over its face, which was most of it.

'Ballbody!' a voice cried from the far end of the table. 'We are ready to begin, if it pleases you.'

Ballbody gathered himself and then launched himself onto the table. Muselings and creatures grabbed at their mugs to pull them out of his way as he rolled along from one end to the other, winking at Alice as he passed. He did not drop into a chair seat (if he had, no one would have been able to see him), but balanced himself on the arm of a chair by an old grey Museling. Mara seated herself on Alice's left; the furry Tove was on her right, his long, twisting nose pointing into the air as he sipped his cocoa which he held in his striped, badger-like paws.

The eldest Museling stood. His fur was black like Mara's, but flecked with grey hairs. ('That is Eling,' whispered Mara.) He looked at each creature in turn for a long moment, and then began speaking in a soft, hoarse old voice.

'I have learned this evening that a diversion has been approved for sometime around midnight. The palace will be busy for at least an hour. Perhaps they will be able to release some of our people. Is now the time? Janya?'

A small, feeble-looking Museling rose and began to recite:

'The fighting hour, when hope has broken into three
    and the child must as the adult be;
The hour of storm, when two birds race
    and blackness grips the full moon's face.'

Every gaze turned slowly towards Alice.

'Perhaps you could tell us a little of your history, child?' the leader asked in a kindly voice.

She was terribly nervous, and kept leaving bits out and having to go back to them. When she told of seeing the Museling on the palace battlements and then finding her in their room, a murmur went round the table; and when she told of the curse that brought the earth crashing over the

cave entrance, shock and anger showed in these good creatures' faces.

Then Mara stood and gave her report. She added that
Phiana was nearly awake again. And then she said something so surprising that Alice's mouth popped open in
astonishment.

'The boy—who is with Dannos—' (cries of 'Good old
Dannos!' and 'Might have guessed it!) 'and I think Casca—'
(laughter and some hand-clapping) 'is well but a little tired.
He will join them in the diversion.'

'Do you know where the older girl is?' Eling asked.

Mara shook her head gravely and sat down.

One of the odd creatures for which Alice could find no
name stood up. The leader nodded, and it began in a high
squeaky voice, 'I was out looking for nuts...' It looked
around at the smiles on the faces of the other creatures
'...as usual. You needn't laugh. If I didn't eat so much I
would disappear altogether.' It squeezed its long thin arms.
Alice now remembered what it reminded her of: it was like a
squirrel, except for the lack of tail.

'As I said, I was out very early—before dawn. I had not
known of these new creatures, and when I met a larger one
of her—' (it nodded timidly at Alice) 'I took fright and
scuttled away. But she was alive then, and in the upper
woods.'

It sat down, and the leader looked about the room. No
one had more to say. He shook his head briefly.

'So, we have the three children—when some had
expected adults, because although the Words speak once of
the young, they speak elsewhere more clearly of the staff in
the hand of one who is full-grown:

> Of grandest stature and fullness of years,
>   for lightning his white hairs;
> And laughter his thunder from other worlds,
>   suddenly he returns—

And you know the rest. We have three children, separated.
Not related, it is true, but all of them children of God. And

tonight brings an eclipse of the full moon. We have no clear knowledge of what the reference to the birds means.'

'Do we start?' It was Feather who spoke, looking around the door to the kitchen. 'I only ask because although you might talk all night about it, there are important things to do—like washing up and making sandwiches!'

The leader looked around those sat at the table. Each in turn nodded at him. Ballbody rolled forward and back in order to nod.

'So we commence. Does anyone have anything else to say?'

'I know a poem,' Ballbody said quickly, 'all about it being the right thyme.

It is Thyme for the Cinna-mon to be Sage.
Don't be a Nut, Meg—and Rosemary, don't rage!
Don't Curry off in a Car, Damon:
Cummin, now, and be forgivin'.
Basil apologised—and he Mint it;
But as for the money, I think he Mustard spent it.'

'Ballbody,' said the leader as the others laughed, 'you're a bit of a nutmeg, yourself. Does anyone have anything *serious* to say? No? Then we go in three hours' time. You all know the plans.'

As they filed out, several creatures nodded to Alice. The tove wriggled away after blurting out its greetings.

Eling walked stiffly to Alice and introduced himself. He was small but upright, standing a head higher than Alice. A scar ran from his right shoulder to his chest.

As she caught sight of this, into her mind flashed a picture of an ancient battle: swords, shouting, the sweat and the sudden anger and bravery of the fight. A flashing blade swept across and back again.

'Yes?' Eling asked. 'You see it, then?' He looked into her eyes for several moments. 'Each one has a past which he holds inside himself. Sometimes the past is written on the outside, too.' He touched his scar. 'But now we look to the future. What do you want to do? You may rest here, and eat and drink and play if you wish.'

'Can't I go with you?'

'It will be dangerous, even for one full-grown.'

'Can't I go?' she repeated. She wanted to stay near them, for safety. The memory of being trapped in the cave was very strong.

'I think you must remain with Ballbody and a few of my people,' Eling began. Seeing Alice's worried frown, he continued: 'Ballbody is perhaps a little odd, for he comes from another place where they do things differently. He was sent to us long ago for our protection, and there are few wiser or braver than he. No one will harm you if he is there.'

She knew it was not right to argue, and she looked down sadly as she agreed: 'I will do as you say, and stay with Ballbody. Please may I go to bed now? I am very tired, and my foot hurts.'

She was taken by Mara to her 'room'. This was a good surprise. Seeing these furry creatures everywhere, she had been fearing a scooped hollow of earth, perhaps lined with a little fur or grass; but there were soft cushions of fragrant straw or heather covered with a quilt in a quiet rocky room, and after finding the wash-rooms she curled onto her bed, pulling a warm down-filled coverlet over her.

She began to drift into a delicious dreaminess. But there was something buzzing in her mind, something she hadn't sorted out yet—now what was it? Was it the difference between black and red Muselings? No, not that. It was so difficult to think clearly. *Oh yes,* she had it now. *Rachel.* They still did not know where Rachel was. With that thought, she fell asleep.

19

Rachel on the Run

It was very black. She waved her hand before her face. Yes, she could just make out the movement. Now, where was she? She rolled onto her side, and then wished she hadn't. She felt sick and numb and desperate all at once. What was wrong? She had been lying here, resting happily on her back, and then....

No, that was all wrong. It began to return to her now. That man—Llama, no Lrans, had been on a horse, and she was on a pony with the others. Lrans had come very close. He had seen her—she saw his expression change to triumph as he peered through the spidery branches in the faint moonlight. Fortunately, the others were too far ahead for him to glimpse.

In a moment of wild decision she decided to lead him back, away from her companions. She rode right at him, then swerved off, avoiding his angry grasp. She tried to think of something rude to shout as she passed, but could do no better than to splutter 'pig-face!' as she plunged down the path.

He caught her just where a shallow stream crossed the path. Coming up on her left, he forced his horse against the pony, and he grabbed the reins out of her hand. They struggled in mid-stream. He threw his other hand across and yanked at her hair. Just then Doc twisted about and bit Lrans hard on the right ankle. Lrans let go of Rachel and, seizing his riding crop, he walloped the pony across the eyes.

That was too much for Rachel. She grabbed his right leg and pushed upwards with all her strength. He had not expected this. Off-balance already, he lost his stirrup on the left side as well, snatched wildly at the air, and went over into the stream with a heavy splash. He swore horribly.

'Come on!' she urged Doc, who sprang forwards. She had the presence of mind to take the reins of Lrans' horse as she passed, and she managed to pull the animal a few hundred yards up the path before losing him. She and Doc left the path and began to wander as quietly as possible, in a direction which she hoped was the right one. They did so for almost an hour.

Doc was going very slowly now. He limped badly. Then he stopped, hanging his head to the ground and breathing unevenly. Rachel panicked. What could she do? She sat without moving for several minutes, sick at heart. Finally, she slipped off and felt his legs in the darkness. The right front was sticky with what she was sure was blood. The horse must have stepped on him in the stream.

She removed the saddle. Then, remembering a little of the horse books she had read, she used the saddle blanket to rub him dry. 'Poor old Doc. We can't have you catching cold.' He rubbed his nose against her.

Just then they had heard the dogs. Something was hunting them. The feeling of panic returned, deepened, and filled her. It was silly, though, because she wasn't at all afraid of dogs—at least, not of small ones. But what if they caught her? What then? She suddenly wanted very much to run, run, not caring where—to run blindly. But she couldn't leave Doc.

Doc, however, seemed to understand. He came over to her and pushed her with his muzzle—hard. He would be all right, he seemed to say. And she realised that Doc was right. They were looking for her, not for the pony.

Using the thin mist of moonlight to guide her in one direction so that she did not simply go round in circles, she set off. For a while the hounds seemed to fall away to her left. Then, suddenly, the noise of baying and scuffling was so great that she was certain they were nearly upon her.

Now she was running, and she could not have stopped running, not until she dropped. Her legs had an urgent, trembling life of their own, and her mind was full of frightening pictures. She must escape, she must get away, she must—how her chest ached, and how sick she felt! She was beginning to cry, and through her tears she saw the moonlight fade while the noise of the dogs still grew.

This chase seemed to go on for ever. Odd thoughts came to her: the old rector, Elias, walking through the woods with a gang of boys; herself, playing netball at school; Alice crying; a fox being pursued to its death by hounds. Her heart was bursting, and in her mind was a sick fear, a frantic anger, and a sound of her own weeping. The noise of dogs seemed to be all around her, and she kept jerking her hands up to her face to save her eyes from their leaping forms, which she imagined at every turn. Then, suddenly, there was nothing under her feet, and water roared in her ears as she fell and the world went hard and black.

And now?

She reopened her eyes and tried to focus on something, anything. A small wind had arisen, reminding her how cold she was. She began to rub her arms and legs with her hands. The ground was damp, and if her cloak had not been of such good quality she would have been soaked through. As it was, her legs and arms had suffered most. Her left arm was numb and might just as well have belonged to someone else.

As she stared about she noticed shadows, and a growing difference between the two corners of the sky. Even now, as she watched, black turned to grey in one direction. So that was East—no, she was thinking of Earth. She did not know which was East here. Her mind became confused with pictures of globes turning clockwise or anti-clockwise, and moons following the turn, but a little more slowly.

She awoke again. The sun was a few inches up from the

horizon. She felt a little better. She pushed herself up onto one elbow, but dropped again to the ground when she heard the noise.

It was a buzzing, humming sound which grew every second. It made her shiver, and she spread herself hard against the ground as it came near. Whatever it was, it travelled at great speed. There was a metallic grinding; then a slowing of speed accompanied by a rise of noise. It was making a growling, squealing sound. Finally, she could bear it no more, and sprang to her feet. She would meet it head on, whatever it was.

The car rounded the bend at the church on Kingsclere Hill, and swept on towards the village, its engine revving.

She sat down again.

From the branches of a nearby beech, a robin looked at her doubtfully. Cats were trouble enough. What was a girl doing on the edge of Flashetts at seven o'clock in the morning? It preened a few feathers, then looked about sharply. It flew away.

20

The Hunt

A moment later, Rachel heard it too: a silvery note blown on a horn about a mile away. The gentry were out fox-hunting early. She stood again, shakily. Wearily, and with much stopping, she went from tree to tree towards the road.

She crossed over and walked along the smaller road to the church gate. Here she halted, and was sick on the grass. Then she felt much better. Yet the pictures of the chase remained in her mind. She saw herself being harried across the countryside, hounds at her heels; imagined again the fear, the tears.

A quiet pad-pad-padding made her turn about, to her right. A small fox was crossing the road. He was reddish, with a little white splash about his tail and muzzle. He was gasping and limping. Rachel's heart went out to him.

She was astonished to see that he did not fear her. Indeed, he ran right up to her and sat on the ground, panting. When she moved through the gate, up the path to the church, he followed. And all the time the horn sounded repeatedly and hounds could be heard baying within the woods. The two fugitives pushed against the round-topped, heavy old church door. It swung open and they went through the inner modern doors as well. The fox scampered up the aisle and hid under the altar cloth at the front. Its claws made a clicking sound on the stony floor.

Rachel closed the door behind her and collapsed into the

nearest pew. She had believed that she was very fit and a fine gymnast; but she was feeble now.

After some minutes, someone from the front of the church began to walk back towards her; there must have been someone else here. She kept her eyes closed. She didn't much care any more. A muffled exclamation hardly made her eyelids flicker. Next she was being picked up by strong arms. They carried her to the children's corner and laid her on the soft cushions there.

The rector returned, bringing water. She sipped it gratefully. His deep, old eyes studied her worriedly. He brushed his few wisps of white hair back from his forehead and stroked his white beard. His wrinkles furrowed even more deeply as he pondered her muddied, exhausted state and her strange clothes. But he said nothing.

Just then, the hounds bayed up the path, and one began scratching at the door. The old man stroked Rachel's hair once, and rose unhurriedly to walk to the door. He was not very tall, being scarcely five and one-half feet high, but he stood straight and proud. Rachel knew his slow walk well— she came every Sunday to church, spurning Sunday School, and hung on his every sermon, though she understood hardly half of them.

He opened the door slowly, shooing away the dogs. They retreated, and a large man took their place, blocking the light in the doorway.

'Ah, Rector! May I come in? Beautiful morning, isn't it?'

The door opened and shut again.

'The fact is, we've tracked some vermin to here—a fox. I expect it slipped in through the door. Just give one of my men a few moments, and we'll flush it out for you.'

'No, thank you,' Elias answered courteously.

'Oh, but—look, Elias—I insist! It will be no trouble to us, I assure you. And there will be no bother or mess. We'll drive the animal out and continue the chase from there.'

'I would rather you didn't, Lord Slarn. I would prefer the creature to live.'

The big man was incredulous. He gaped at the small old fellow. Then he smiled.

'Come now, Rector, I'm a good churchman like yourself. I pay my dues. I do my bit for the people, and for the village, and for the countryside. I don't chase foxes for cruelty, but to protect the countryside. Foxes are vermin— they are dirty creatures who kill chickens and ducks and pheasants.'

'So do you.'

'What?'

'Lord Slarn, you also kill chickens, ducks and pheasants. But I do not mount a horse and attempt to chase you to your death. I allow you to find your own way to that place. The fox is also one of God's creatures. Will you not leave him in peace?'

The big man's jaw dropped. His smile drooped. His red coat swished as he turned about and stalked out. At the door he turned back. 'I won't forget this, Reverend. You won't find it easy to justify this before the council.'

The old man simply bowed. The door slammed. He turned and walked towards the altar. Halfway, he knelt in the aisle.

The fox poked its nose out under the cloth. Then it crept slowly up the aisle until it reached the old man. It sat before him. After a few minutes Elias sighed, and stretched out his arm to pat the creature lightly.

'Well, brother fox. And what are we to do with you? I can't take you to live in the rectory. I can't leave you here. I can't let you go.'

Rachel crept out and walked to him.

'Can't he come with me to the Home?' she asked.

'No, dear girl. I'll have to carry him out in secret some time, Rachel, and put him back in the woods. I wish I could take him right out of the world, for they will catch him one day. Look—he cannot run fast enough to escape the hounds, because he has a twisted foot.'

'Like Alice.'

'That reminds me. Where is Alice? And Robert? And

where have you been? The village has been looking for you these three days, but not a sign have we had of you.'

'Three days? But she said that time would not pass so quick here as there. She said....' Rachel's voice trailed off. They had been tricked. Or had they? Was it a dream? Were Alice and Robert somewhere in Flashetts? She was suddenly uncertain about the difference between truth and stories.

'Come with me. We'll go back to the rectory for some breakfast, and you can tell me all.'

'But what about the fox?'

'I'll lock him in the vestry, as I usually do. I'll bring him some water, and I keep a little food for him, near the Communion bread.'

They walked along the empty road. If the hunters had left any spies, they were well hidden. On this summer morning, only the birds seemed to be about. Several crows were on the cricket field opposite the church; sparrows were arguing about a worm one of them had discovered on the pavement; swallows swung across the skies after the early morning midges.

The rectory was a large brick building, made for an expanding family with servants. Elias Jones lived there alone, as he had done for ten years. He pushed the creaking wooden garden gate open, then held it for her and refastened it with a length of old cord before preceding her through the sleepy, bee-heavy, poppy-covered lawn to his back door. An apple tree leaned over them as he turned the key.

Within a few minutes the kettle was on and Rachel was asleep in a chair. But she was only cat-napping, and a cup of coffee with a muffin vanished soon after it was put before her; then another; then another.

Between mouthfuls, she told Elias everything she could recall: the tree, the palace, the horse ride, the creatures, the flight at night, the chase, and the feelings she'd had. Elias said little, except to encourage her to recall exactly what was said and done. What precisely did she feel about the

Queen, about Lrans, about Heck, about the Muselings?
What colour was the Museling?

Only when she mentioned the crow's name did he start
up, his eyes suddenly alight. He smiled wryly. 'Ahab...and
Jess, you said...yes, it makes sense now.' But what it was
that made sense, he would not say. He asked permission to
tell the Home that she was back.

'I don't want to go back to the Home yet. I want to get
back to the others.'

'I can see that. But the Home should know that you are
here and are well. You can stay with me today. Tonight you
must go back there. Tomorrow—well, tomorrow I can take
our friend back to the wood. Perhaps you will come with
me?' He winked at her as he said it. 'We can look at trees,
you know. Once one knows the right tree, who knows what
one can do?'

'Why can't we go now?'

He held out his hands expressively. 'Because I have
promised to visit an old woman in hospital. She will not live
long, and it is my duty to guide her to God. Tomorrow I am
free. Will you wait that long?'

Suddenly Rachel felt exhausted. She nodded.

'Come—have a lie-down in the front room. I'll close the
curtains. A sleep will do you good.' He led her through to
the other room, and returned with pillows and covers. By
this time she was fast asleep. He saw to it that she was
comfortable, and tiptoed out to his study. He opened his
Bible to the book of Kings.

'I may as well refresh my memory. One forgets so much.'

21

The Home

When Rachel woke in the late afternoon, she knew immediately where she was. This was a relief; it had been horribly confusing to open her eyes each morning and stare with surprise into unfamiliar surroundings. She lay, happy and lazy, on the couch. The rectory was not home, but she had often been there for meetings—a small solemn fairy among the talkative adults. More recently she had felt secure enough to join in the discussions. It annoyed her that the adults were surprised to hear her say things that were sensible. Why did adults think children were stupid?

She heard the gate creak open, then shut. It was someone heavy—there were firm footfalls, and the sound of large puffy breaths. Rachel closed her eyes. It could only be Mrs Welter. The noise of sharp knocking confirmed her suspicions. Then Mrs Welter's clear, rounded and uninterruptable voice poked through the walls: 'I met Audrey in the village, and she happened to mention she saw you with Rachel when she was on her way to the mill—Audrey, that is, not the girl. At least, she thought it was Rachel. She was in a hurry. You know how she hurries....'

Finally, Rector Jones led the woman into the front room.

'Well, young lady, and where have you been? Wanted a holiday, did you? I don't suppose you considered the trouble we'd all suffer—hunting for you in the woods, looking in the river—'

Rachel opened her eyes and saw Mrs Welter standing with her hands firmly on her hips.

'I am sorry—'

'And phoning round the police stations. Where are the others? Camping in the woods, like last time? I don't know why you can't camp in the back garden; it's large enough.'

'We didn't mean to cause—'

'Mr Welter has been awake past midnight some nights for worry that you might come back and find the door locked.'

'Mrs Welter—'. The Rector held up his hand. 'Rachel has said she is sorry. And she is quite exhausted. Perhaps you could let her stay here for the day? I will bring her round this evening.'

'No, Rector. I couldn't do that. She's my responsibility. Mr Welter and myself, we look upon ourselves as her parents. It's as if she was our own child, and we must look after her. You wouldn't separate a child from her mother, would you?'

'Well—that depends on the child and the mother. But it is Rachel's health I am thinking of. A little rest would do her good.'

Mrs Welter frowned. Rachel knew that frown, and knew also what it meant when Mrs Welter squeezed her plump hands hard together in annoyance. With a sigh, Rachel slipped from the settee and stood a little unsteadily.

'I'm all right, really. I'll go home with Mrs Welter. I need a bath anyway.'

The old man smiled at her. 'Perhaps I will see you tomorrow, then?' He winked from behind Mrs Welter's back, and held up six fingers, for six o'clock. Rachel nodded.

'Thank the Rector for his kindness,' prompted Mrs Welter.

'Thank you, Elias.'

Mrs Welter frowned again, but said nothing. She did not hold with ministers being called anything but 'Rector' or 'Vicar', and she was not happy with children calling adults by their first names. She turned on her heel, said, 'Thank you, Rector,' and shepherded Rachel out of the house.

Once out the gate, Rachel felt a sudden wildness come upon her. Given the slightest push, she would have skitted off up the hill, dodging through the graveyard among the tombstones, leaving Mrs Welter puffing far behind, a small speck in the distance—no, not a *small* speck, Mrs Welter could never be one of those.

However, the thought that she *could* escape if she wished, and the image in her mind of Mrs Welter squeezing through the gate and pursuing her tortoise-like through the churchyard, satisfied her for the time. It was nearly as good to think of escape as to attempt it. Mrs Welter, who was quite quick-witted when she was not talking, guessed that Rachel was considering escape and wisely said nothing to her until they reached the house; then she motioned in the direction of the bathroom and puffed: 'When you've had your bath, the doughnuts should be ready.'

This small statement banished all ideas of flight from Rachel's mind; and Mrs Welter knew it. She never bought doughnuts, but made them herself. You ate them hot, while drinking cocoa. They were a Saturday treat usually, but at other times they could be a powerful tool for cheering up a dismal child or winning over a rebellious one. Besides that, Mrs Welter loved them herself, and welcomed any opportunity to take out the deep fat frier, mix up the creamy doughy batter, and prepare batch after batch of soft, heavenly golden rings, sprinkled with icing sugar.

The tactic worked now, as it usually did. Between mouthfuls, a clean Rachel was soon telling Mrs W about where she had been, and what had been happening to them for the last three days. Mrs W did not believe her, of course; but she was too wise to show that. And Rachel did not believe that Mrs W believed her; but she, too, was wise enough to hide the fact.

Therefore, an hour later, Mrs W was able to say to a local policeman that the other two were most definitely hiding in the wood somewhere, as they had hidden before, and it was no use trying to persuade Rachel to talk—the girl had invented some wonderful cock-and-bull story from which she couldn't be shifted. The policeman listened respectfully, and went back to the station in Whitchurch. He had known Mrs Welter long enough to trust her. Children were always running away from the Home; who could blame them? But they always returned—the food was too good to miss, and they knew that the Welters actually liked them rather than just 'putting up' with them.

For her part, Rachel was relieved beyond measure. She had told the truth, and it had not led to her being sent to her room, or shouted at: unfortunately, that is what adults sometimes do even when you are completely honest with them. Mr Welter had once asked her whether she didn't think Mrs Welter was just the right shape for a woman, and Rachel had said that she was more the right shape for a balloon. She had had to spend the whole day in her room for that, and had missed her doughnuts the next Saturday.

At last the clock edged past 3 pm. The other children would arrive soon, after a day at 'summer school'—for one week in August, school opened and there were games, art and swimming. From the back garden, Rachel heard Mrs W put the kettle on the stove, and then there was a clatter of plates and thump of a bread-board onto the worktop. Lunch had been sandwiches and salad. This would be bread and jam with cupcakes (home-made), washed down by strong milky tea.

One set of agile footsteps after another announced the arrival of the other four orphans. A boy's head, sprouting spikey orange hair, poked out from the upstairs playroom window. 'Watcher, Rach! Did yer get far?'

'Halfway 'cross the universe!'

'Bet yer didn't even make Basingstoke.'

She cupped one hand behind her ear—the signal that Mrs W was within earshot. The head disappeared, but one of the teddy bears flew out of the window a few seconds later, narrowly missing her. She threw it back, and the game continued until Mrs W shouted for them. Her voice was amazing. You could sometimes hear her from the other side of the village.

After eating, the five of them held a meeting to hear about Rachel's adventures. They always did this, and those who had run away would recount their progress with great pride. Nobby, who was a little older than Rachel, had once gone all the way to Manchester before having to give himself up because he'd had nothing to eat for days. He was the leader of the group—a rough boy who knew how to fight and who had often been in trouble for it. Now he sat openmouthed as Rachel detailed her journeys to him and the other three boys.

Unlike Mrs W, they believed her. They expected her to exaggerate a little—after all, they would do so themselves—but they were easily convinced that most of her journey was true. Rachel's adventures were no more unbelievable than a lot they learned at school. And, given a choice between believing Rachel or believing their teachers, they would have chosen Rachel every time.

'So what're you goin' to do?' asked Nobby. The other three, all around seven years old, nodded in agreement with the question.

'Well—the one thing I didn't tell Whaley was that I'm meeting the rector at six tomorrow morning, and we're trying to find the tree then. Oh—and to find the fox a home. I forgot to tell you about the hounds. They were chasing him, see, there in Flashetts.'

The full telling of the history took over an hour, with many pauses for repeats.

'Tell us about the fight again. What'd 'e say when you pushed him off?' one of the younger ones asked, gazing at her with reverence.

'Hold on, Rach,' interrupted Nobby. 'Why can't we come back with yer? It must be better'n school! And we could help find the others.'

'I don't know...we'd better ask Elias. He'd know what was right.'

They nodded solemnly. Sometimes they did not understand much of what the old man said in church, but they liked him and were in awe of him. His sparse white hair about his bald dome, and his long white beard put them in mind of a prophet in the Bible who had called the bears down upon the disrespectful children. True, there were no bears in Overton; but they half-believed some would materialise if the old man called for any.

'Yeah—the Rev will know what to do.'

'Yeah.'

'Yer. But we'll 'ave to see to it that Whaley don't wake up. You'll do the business, won't yer, Simey? She'll never see *you* in the dark.'

Simon, a thin black boy, nodded, grinning. Whenever they needed to ensure that the Welters overslept, it was his job to creep into their bedroom after midnight and disable the clock by switching off the alarm and winding the hands back an hour or so.

'You're just jealous,' he answered with pride. The others nodded. Any of the boys would have given a lot to be as quick as Simey was about the Home or on the football field.

'What'cha reckon, then? D'we need supplies?' asked Nobby.

'I think so, Nobby. Some bread would come in useful, anyhow. Maybe some cheese and something to drink.'

Half an hour later Mrs Welter was staring into the larder. She must have used more bread at tea-time than she'd thought. There was still time to walk down to the shops in the village. She'd pick up some more juice, too, and some cheese and pickles—and a couple of packets of biscuits. It was astonishing what they managed to get through in the space of a few days. Now, where had that shopping bag gone to?

22

Alice Plays a Part

It must have been around two o'clock in the morning when Alice woke from a dreamless sleep. Ballbody was just inside the door, bouncing a little.

'You must get up!' he whispered. 'And get dressed as quick as you can. There's mischief about.' His voice was low and round and muffled, as though he spoke from inside a large suet pudding.

She slipped out of bed and threw on her clothes, which had been cleaned and dried. Pulling trainers onto her feet, she watched the round creature who stood in the doorway, politely looking out into the dimly lighted corridor.

'I'm ready now.'

He signalled her to follow, and rolled off down the tunnel like a runaway cricket ball. She had to walk swiftly to match his pace. Soon they were going up a gentle incline, and a cooler air was playing about the passage. Then the light changed as the moon cast its eeriness into the mouth of the exit. With a few more steps they were outside. A thin mist had wetted the trees and now hung about them. The hazy moon was one-third of the way into the sky. Only a few bright stars penetrated the mist.

The tunnel came out into thick brush, through which Alice could walk only by bending double and ducking beneath the more tangled branches. In this fashion she struggled her way to the top of a gentle rise, envying Ballbody who cheerfully rolled through the thicket. He was not altogether quiet while he did this; he hummed a tune which was interrupted from time to time by a sudden small 'Oh!' as he rolled over a particularly thorny bramble or a nettle.

At last they came out of the underbrush, and Ballbody now signalled her to be quiet. They were looking down from the hilltop at a wide grassland upon which the moon shone murkily.

'Over to your left,' Ballbody murmured.

She stared for some moments. What she saw was a moving pattern of light, like sunshine seen through the branches of trees blown by a gentle breeze. Then the patterns took on meaning: she could see a horse, then several horses and many people, carrying things. By the way they held these 'things', it was clear that they were weapons of various types. They were still far off—perhaps a mile.

'What is it?'

'An attack of some sort, I am sure. They are coming this way, and for no good reason.'

'And what should we do?'

Ballbody peered hard at the coming force, then swivelled round to look in the opposite direction. He was muttering to himself.

'Ballbody!'

'What? Oh, pardon, I was working something out. You see, the city is over *there*,' (he pointed by nodding his head forwards and a little to his right towards a vague glow beyond a belt of trees), 'but the army is over *here*.' He pointed to the left. 'They aren't going back to the city, but are coming in our direction.'

'Do they know about the tunnels?'

'Oh yes...have done for years. But they would never have tried to attack, not if it meant going underground...at least, not until now.'

'What can we do?' she asked again.

He was silent for a few seconds. Then, as if he had been bitten by an insect, he gasped suddenly and jumped into the air.

'The factory!' he cried. 'They are coming from the factory! It all makes sense now—and—heaven help us—they will be here in a few minutes. You must go and warn the others.'

'Me?' Her face went hot, and her heart began to thump. She suddenly felt sick.

'You. I must stay here and do what I can. Run for the city. Use the forest road; the others will be returning that way if they have started back. Tell them about the army. Tell them to expect an ambush at the tunnel.' He said all this in a hurried whisper.

'What road?' She tried to answer calmly, but the words came out in a squeak.

He nodded towards the belt of trees. 'Look down from the moon to the forest, then a little to the right. You'll see a break in the trees. Go for that, and you'll find a narrow road. It leads all the way to the city. But you must go now. And run! And keep your head down until you are out of sight of the army—your fair hair can be seen for miles. Now—go!'

Alice shut her mouth tight against the protests she had been about to make and, bending low, began to scramble down the hillside, keeping in the shade of trees where she could. She had been about to say that she would stay with Ballbody, and that she was too little to run all the way to the city, and that...that she was afraid to go into the dark wood alone. But Ballbody's urgency had driven her down the hill. She wiped sudden tears from her eyes as she went. She was horribly angry with someone or something—no, perhaps not angry at all, except with herself. She was crying because she was frightened, and she was angry because she hated being frightened.

It had looked a short run down to the woods; but distances down a hill or in the dark usually seem shorter than they are, and this stumbling journey proved quite long. Before she reached the woods she was aware of new noises behind her, but she was too frightened to turn and look. Finally she reached the margin of the wood. She stopped, gasping with effort and fear. At this end of the road, the trees grew over the path, screening out the light of the moon and stars. Blackness opened before her, like the blackness within the huge jaws of some monstrous snake lying on the ground.

She could not go forwards, and turned to look back. The soldiers were moving into the hillside thicket she had left. Some carried large, oddly-shaped packs on their backs, and others were pulling small carts whose wheels rattled and squealed. Suddenly a scuffle broke out, and a small round object shot through their midst, upsetting one of the carts. It rolled down the hill, slanting away from the path Alice had taken. Several soldiers ran off after it.

Go, Ballbody! Alice whispered to herself. She looked back to her own dark path. She sighed and began a cautious shuffle inside the mouth of the 'snake'.

Once inside, she found that her eyes got used to the darkness within a few minutes. Soon she was jogging along the path—not happily, but at least not so miserably as when she had entered the wood. For almost half an hour she alternately walked and ran. The road dipped and crossed a shallow stream which soaked her to the knees. It then climbed up, broadened, and bore round to the right. The trees fell back from the road and she ran in hazy moonlight. Something was tugging at her memory. She glanced about, then looked down at the clay path from which a warm fine dust arose as she trotted along. Of course—this was the very path they had stood by and watched the Queen process along, that first day. Somewhere to her left, the Muselings had been. To the right—

Her heart went terribly cold. There were eyes in the woods. Large ones, small ones... some of them moved along as she did. And every few yards she caught sight of yet another pair of yellow, green or red orbs glinting in the moonlight. Even worse than these were the eyes which did not come in pairs, but appeared singly. She put her head down and ran hard, concentrating on the road. Left, right, left, right, left....

For several minutes she managed not to look around. In some ways this was worse. She imagined the eyes coming closer, and long thin tentacles or clawing arms shooting out from the wood, snatching at her as she passed. When she looked up, however, it was not towards the woods. Something had caught her attention directly before her, up in the air. Darkness blurred the face of the moon, accompanied by a faint swishing sound. She knew at once what it was: Ahab was on the wing.

Then she saw that the dark blur was growing larger and had become two blurs. She stopped, aghast. There could be no doubt. Two winged creatures, hideously outlined against the faint light of moon and stars, were coming straight towards her. For a moment she stood stupidly in the middle of the road, before she realised that they would surely see her there. Automatically she started for the protection of the woods. She stopped as she saw the eyes. She glanced back up the road. The creatures were bearing down on her swiftly.

Catching her breath in horror, Alice shot suddenly into the wood. She was more afraid of the crows than the eyes— but only slightly more afraid. She threw herself onto the ground and covered her head with her hands. There was a double whoosh as the creatures glided past, their wings almost touching the tops of the trees. She lay still until the noise of them had almost faded away. There were other noises too—noises nearer at hand. When at last she looked up, it was to find a pair of eyes within a foot of her own.

The rabbit (or some creature very like one) hopped a little nearer, and looked at her hopefully. Relieved, she sat up and laughed, tears running down her face. Three small furry animals, warm and roly-poly and with only one eye each, waddled up and tried to climb onto her lap. A deer peered at her with nervous eyes from behind a tree. Other creatures, all of them apparently of a kindly nature, stood or sat in the shadows.

Her legs were shaking too much from her fright for her to move just yet, so she spent some minutes stroking any creatures brave enough to come within reach. The one-eyed 'fuzzies', as she called them, purred like kittens in her lap, and strange thin animals shaped like small horses timidly licked her hands and rubbed their furry muzzles against her feet. Perhaps this was what paradise had been like—she could imagine Eve calling the creatures to her, going for a ramble in the woods, inviting them into the Garden of Eden for a bowl of milk and a stroke.

At last her conscience whispered to her, and she rose to go. The fuzzies mewed about her feet as she left the wood. They would not venture onto the path though, and scooted back into the woods when she recommenced her run.

Now she looked eagerly for the eyes in the woods. It was like being a runner trying for a prize, with a crowd urging you on to go faster, and faster yet. Her legs stretched out, pulling her on at a pace she had not known she could run. Her bad foot ached, but she found that she could bear the pain. The road climbed again, but she kept her speed, cheered on by an audience which mewed, whistled, barked, lowed or simply blinked its eyes at her as she passed.

Soon she was at the end of the wood—and she quickly nipped among the trees again, to the right. A line of people, or creatures, was walking along the left-hand border of the woods. She waited quietly behind a tree. If they were Muselings, all was safe...but she was suddenly disappointed. The first to come into view was a grim-looking lad with a dirty face, leading a burdened horse and peering suspiciously about him. This must be yet another army of the Queen's soldiers. *Wait a minute....*

Before the lad could leap aside, he saw a small yellow-haired creature dash out from a tree and throw itself at him.

'Alice!'

'Rob! It's you! You're safe! And me—'

'Well, I can see that! What're you doing here? Where's Rach? No, you wouldn't know either.'

Hurriedly she began to tell him about the army, but he stopped her.

'You'd better tell the others. Dannos!'

Dannos, in fact, had only been a few steps away. Robert had not noticed him come up, so excited had he been suddenly to see Alice again.

'At your side, Boy-with-an-earthquake-for-a-voice. The Queen in her palace can probably hear you.'

'This is Alice.'

Dannos bowed. 'I am honoured. Wobbit's friend is mine.' He held out his paw and Alice slapped it firmly.

'Listen, Tannos,' she began.

'Dannos!'

'Dannos, then. I have a message for all of you.' Hurriedly she told them all that Ballbody had said. 'And there are two crow-like things about.'

Dannos held a hurried discussion with a small group of Muselings. Then he rushed off without another word. Haste was essential.

Alice asked, 'And, please, where are the other Muselings? I mean, the ones who were in the tunnels with me. Mara and the others.'

'They're back in the city, makin' a few adjustments to the factories. Ruby won't be makin' any more perfume for a while.' This was Casca, who had come up out of the shadows.

'Ruby?' Alice was puzzled. 'And what perfumes?'

'Come on,' said Robert. 'I'll explain as we go.'

'Go where?'

Casca waved at the dark trees. 'Into the forest. Danny's goin' back to tell the others, an' we'll go find a good place for a picnic and a kip. Come in careful, though, and mind the Rollies cos' they're allus tryin' to be used as footballs.' He pointed at a little group of 'fuzzies' which had gathered around Alice's legs.

'C'mon, Ghostie!' Casca said to Robert.

'Ghostie?' asked Alice.

Robert grinned. 'Yeah—I'll explain that too. But not until you tell me how you got here.'

It was all going to take a lot of explanation.

23

Full House

It was raining hard. Five pairs of feet splashed through the rivulets that rushed down the hill towards the church. Water squelched in their shoes and ran from their heads in bright streams, but the children laughed as they ran. There is something about being drenched by rain that cleans the soul and livens the heart.

Nobby, Rachel, Simey, Daz and Gwil weren't worried in the least about getting soaked, but only about getting to the church at the agreed time. The rain was a bonus. It broke the mad heat of the summer and settled the gritty dust the cars had kicked onto the hedges and pavement. They stamped water at one another and shook wild showers from their hair. The Reverend Elias, waiting at the church gate, nodded to them as they scampered up to him with wet smiles on their faces. He had half a mind to dance in the cool water himself.

'And then there were six,' he said pleasantly.

'D'you mind, Elias? They want to come as well if you say it's all right.'

'We'll be no trouble—promise, Rev, cross my heart.... That's right, boys, innit?' Nobby added.

The others mumbled their agreement, looking up shyly at the rector.

'I think...I think that it is very important that you mean what you say. Will you follow orders if that becomes necessary?'

'Whatever you say, Rev.'

'We'll be white as snow.'

''Cept for Simey, of course. Ow!'

There was a pause as Simey and Daz set on Gwil and tickled him until he took back what he'd said. Then Simey added: 'We'll be terribly, terribly good.'

'Come on, then, all of you.' Elias took his walking staff from the churchyard wall, turned towards the church and whistled softly. A red form sped down the pebbled path and followed at the old man's heels as they continued down the hill.

'His foot is better!' exclaimed Rachel.

'A little. Let's cross the road.'

They entered the wood. The trees looked different in the rain: they seemed to stand more upright and spread their branches more widely, like men rising and stretching after a long languid doze in soft armchairs.

'That's the one we went in—the oak.'

They gathered about it, prodding its gnarled bark and clambering over its protruding roots.

'There was a pattern in the bark, but it's gone now. Perhaps the rain hides it. Still, it was just here. Rob was pushing it.'

The children spent some time tugging and pressing and twisting, but managed only to break off some of the bark. Elias stood and watched, deep in thought. Rain dripped from his beard as from the moss above their heads.

'I give up. It'll not open, look.'

The others reluctantly agreed. They looked about glumly.

'What'll we do, then, Rev?'

'We will go for a walk. Perhaps we are looking too hard.'

So they walked for a few minutes in silence. The fox trotted on before them, like a dog leading its masters on a trail it knew well. Following him, they left the main path and plunged into wilder woods. Brambles tore at their trousers and scratched their hands. The rain dripped from the branches high overhead.

When the fox halted, they stopped too. It was darker here, and quiet. Blocking their progress was a twenty-foot strip of stinging nettles and brambles which choked a humped chalky wasteland. Behind it rose a large bank, twice their height. They knew that beyond this bank was a field, and beyond that the main road. Brambles climbed the steep bank in places, and their thorny branches hung in spiky waterfalls from the chalky soil. The fox began to push in among the nettles.

'Come on then. What are you waiting for?'

'In there? An' get nettled all over?'

But Simey boldly followed the fox's lead, and then the others. Elias came last, parting the nettles with his staff. Close to the bank, under the hanging brambles, they wound through the sea of nettles which were sometimes over their heads. It was dreadful. They were stung by the flapping leaves and tormented by gnats which flew at their heads. Just as Rachel was about to turn back, she heard Simey shout. She ran ahead and found him standing at the mouth of a small cave.

It could hardly be called a cave. It was a hole in the bank about two feet wide and four high. You could see through it to the other side—there were more nettles, high grass, hanging brambles, and trees beyond. Disappointed, she turned back and told the others that it didn't go anywhere. They pressed around her and looked through the hole as well, shaking their heads at the thought of yet more nettles and brambles.

Elias stared long into the opening. 'You all seem to have missed something rather important. Look again.'

They did, but there was nothing very important about nettles and blackberry bushes. Finally, Daz, who was the smallest, said timidly, 'It—it ain't rainin' in there, is it?'

'Brilliant! Through you go, then. And where's that fox? Already gone through? Well, he had more sense than the lot of us. Come on, Nobby! A few more nettle stings won't hurt you much!'

'Yer an 'ard one, Rev. Why don't you go first and knock 'em all down wiv yer stick?'

'I didn't think of that, Nobby. Shall I go first, then?'

A few swipes flattened the nettles about the hole. Elias then had to bend almost double to squeeze through the entrance. The tunnel was around six feet long, and within a minute they had all pushed their way into the field on the other side. Their clothes were muddy, and there was mud in their hair. They wiped their hands on the grass, which took over from the nettles within a few feet of the tunnel's exit. They were in a small wood.

'It's dry—the grass is dry!'

'Is this the same place, Rach?'

She shrugged her shoulders. They might be anywhere. The fox cub trotted up and sat at her feet, panting happily in the sunshine.

They looked about them, and finally began walking towards the place where the trees appeared to be thinnest. The sun was before them, wrapped in an early-morning haze. There was something odd about this wood—but for several minutes none of them could identify it.

'This place feels strange.'

'Yeah—it's like a graveyard.'

'Quiet, innit?'

'Too quiet, Dazzy. I don't like it.'

'Stop!' Rachel cried suddenly. 'I know where we are. We've got to go back.'

'Where are we, then?' asked Elias. He was leaning against a tree, his brow wrinkled and a frown on his face. He, too, felt that there was something unusual about the silence.

'We're near Ahab's lair. See—we've come uphill and there's a crown of trees about the summit just ahead, and I can see those nasty flowers sparkling just beyond. That's why there's no animals about.'

'Let's turn round, then,' suggested Gwil. It was the first time he had spoken that day; he had been too frightened to say anything at all since they left the churchyard.

They all muttered agreement except for the old man, who stood peering ahead.

'What do you say, Elias?' asked Rachel.

He sighed. 'I think I must go to the summit. If I do not go now, I will have to go later: and that might be too late. Will any of you come with me?'

They all looked down. Rachel blushed; she knew he was looking at her. But she said nothing.

He immediately apologised, 'It was wrong for me to ask. But do this for me: run as quickly as you can for the place where Rachel first met the Muselings. Can you find the spot, Rachel?'

'I—I think so. I can see the road from here, and it should be along that.'

'Then go—immediately! Find them and say that I am here. And don't stop for any reason. And keep out of danger if you can. No heroics.'

'Will you be all right, Rev?'

'No, Daz, I don't think I will—but there are worse things than danger and death! I have been a coward once in my life. This is the time to put it right. Now—goodbye!'

He turned suddenly and began to climb the steep portion of the hill. The others stared after him stupidly. They had never known him to be so abrupt, or so agitated.

24

Battle Commences

'C'mon, everyone.' A despondent Rachel led the group down the hill and to their right. She felt that she should have offered to go with Elias. Even though she couldn't have done very much, she should have offered. But the memory of that beast clawed at her insides. If only she hadn't had those dreams, hadn't seen the Museling grasped in those cruel talons, hadn't seen those cold, fearful eyes.

She led them to the road. They were dry now. The mud rubbed off their clothes as powdery dirt, and their gym shoes had lost their squelch. A fine dust—red and dry—rose from their footsteps.

'Look, Rach! Someone's been 'ere afore us!'

'Yeah, there's footprints—small ones, too. Wearin' gym shoes, too, d'you think?'

They all bent over the prints. No one imagined that they were the tracks made by Alice running in the dark along this road just a few hours before. They continued, following the trail with interest. As they did, they became aware of a distant noise—like the noise of bees humming in a garden, mixed with the rattle of pans in the kitchen. This puzzled them and made them hurry for the next few minutes.

Cries, shouts and sudden howls and screams greeted them. The noise grew until, rounding a bend, they saw the explanation for it laid out before them like a completed jigsaw puzzle lying on a table.

The road came to the end of the wood within a hundred

yards of them. Choking the road were soldiers—many soldiers, dressed in the white and scarlet colours of the Queen. The Queen herself was among them, waving a sword and shouting threats and encouragement. Over the woods to the right hung a white vapour, and from this quarter advanced the Muselings and a host of other creatures.

The creatures were mostly unarmed. They fought with claws and teeth against the swords and knives, throwing themselves on their attackers. The soldiers had all the advantages—tough uniforms for protection, weapons of steel, and cannisters of a sickening gas which they threw into the woods. With horror, Rachel saw Robert crawl out from among the trees, his face white. He had been gassed and was coughing. He was sick on the ground.

'Stones!' shouted Nobby above the noise. Rachel grimly snatched the largest one she could throw and ran straight at the battle. In the ten seconds it took to come within range, she had chosen her target. Rather, the target had chosen itself. The Queen had sighted Robert, and was urging her horse through the battling crowd towards him. Her eye was bent on him with a horrible bright vengeance, and she was blind to all else.

She rode to within a few feet of him, and flashed a triumphant, snarling smile at his pale, shaking face.

'A ghost, are you? Perhaps you enjoyed your joke. But now, young man, the joke is on you. A ghost you will be, and no mistake.' She lifted her hand, as she had done at the cave. Robert did not flinch. Instead, and for the second time in six hours, he stuck his tongue out at her. She flushed scarlet and, mad with rage, reached instead for her sword. But her hand never touched it. A stone came whirring through the acrid air and struck her full in the face. Before she could whirl about, another followed. A lanky, fair girl with tears streaming down her cheeks threw a handful of sand into her eyes and rushed upon her, grabbing her leg.

The Queen kicked out, but Rachel held and bit hard at the ankle which struck her in the face. The horse neighed and rose into the air. The Queen swung the whip she held in her right hand, intending to strike Rachel across the eyes. Rachel ducked, and the blow caught the horse on its neck. It bolted, carrying the Queen back into the battle. Here she was set upon by Muselings and was forced back to the rear. On the way she lost her sword, torn from her grasp by an immensely tall, black-furred female Museling. The Museling twisted the sword in her hands until it bent double, and threw it into the trees. Weaponless, the Queen took fright and sent her horse galloping madly away.

Rachel did not see any of this. She ran to Robert and hugged him.

He smiled wanly. 'What took you so long?' he asked, and tried to laugh. It made him cough terribly.

'Can I do anything for you?'

'Water. Please.' He nodded to some flasks nearby. The battle had rolled back onto the other side of the road, leaving men and creatures fallen on this side. Discarded flasks and other items littered the ground. Rachel snatched one up, and he drank from it greedily. She glanced around.

The orphans had made quite a difference to the battle. They would gather stones and come in for bombing raids, with painful accuracy. Then they slipped quickly out of range of the swords. Soldiers who did not keep an eye on the four boys soon felt a rock on the head. Those who did try to watch the urchins couldn't pay full attention to the attacking creatures. Either way, they were put off their stroke, and many of them now found themselves swordless. These soldiers quickly surrendered rather than fight against animals that could bite and scratch so fiercely. A group of them now stood prisoners in the shadow of the woods on the same side as Rachel and Robert.

'Where's Alice?'

Robert pointed beyond the battle and to the right. The Queen, too, had her prisoners. Alice sat sulkily on a boulder, her hands tied before her. She did not appear to be injured. A soldier stood at her side, guarding her and a few other creatures.

Rachel became aware now that there was more of the

battle which she could not see, away to the left beyond the edge of the trees. The shouting that rose from this corner was more noticeable now because most of the soldiers in the road had surrendered. With the shouts came other noises— screeching cries and sharp, shrill calls. Then two shapes rose above the trees and bore down on the battle in the road.

Rachel suddenly understood why the Queen's army could not be defeated. Ahab was there, and with him was another of his kind. The two crow-beasts flew upon the Muselings, pecking and clawing. The Muselings had to give way, and one of them fell. The crows veered off, passing Rachel as they did. She started. The first was Ahab, certainly; but the second—the second crow's eyes—no, it was crazy, but they reminded her of the eyes of the choir lady who had taken the flower.

The crows banked to the right, levelled, and began their descent again, heading for Nobby and his band. The four of them bravely grabbed for stones to hurl; but they would have no chance against these monsters. The crows were less than fifty yards away...twenty...ten.

Ahab cawed suddenly. He swept up and over Rachel's head, ignoring Simey's stone, which caught him in the side. The other crow followed. They sped like two arrows across the trees, back the way which Rachel and the boys had come. Rachel and Rob stared after them. Two miles distant, the hill of flowers stood above the trees. From this hill rose a black smoke. It was ablaze with a fierce and unusual fire. White, red and green sparks shot into the air, and their eerie lights traced an arching path to the ground just as if they were fireworks on the Fifth of November.

The remaining soldiers stared, aghast. Then, realising their situation, they slowly lowered their swords and dropped them to the ground. They placed their hands on their heads to show that they surrendered.

The only soldier who hesitated was the one guarding the Queen's prisoners. The Queen turned her eye on him and pointed to Alice.

'Kill her!'

The unhappy guard raised his sword. But he dropped it again and shook his head. The Queen, scowling and livid, rode him down and snatched Alice onto her saddle. Within a few seconds they had fled far down the road towards the castle.

25

Robert's Story

'Go on, Rob—tell us what she said.'

They were marching to the palace. About them were more than a hundred creatures, mostly Muselings. Rob had paused in his tale to cough. His cheeks were pink again, but his throat felt most unpleasant.

'She said something rude. You should've heard her, Nobby. I didn't think queens swore. I didn't know half the words but all of them was terrible. It was a shock for her, see? Findin' all her prisoners gone, and then being told she was to leave the place or else.'

The listeners tried to imagine the occasion: the Queen coming to the palace door at dawn to be met by the eldest Museling bearing a flag of truce. Behind him had been a small group of creatures, including two humans. She had started at the sight of Robert and Alice. Her great hands clenched and unclenched. Her face reddened. When the old grey leader, Eling, delivered his command that she leave their land, she flung foul oaths in his face.

Robert continued: 'Then she said, "I promise you one thing only, old fool, and that is a slow death. You cannot withstand me. Even the prophet ran from me like a dog, and you are no prophet." '

'The wot?'

'I'm tellin' you what she said, Daz, not what I understand. Anyway, she laughed in a nasty way an' started some sort of spell, so we went out quick as quick.'

'How d'you know it was a spell?'

'Cos it was all words of a nasty sort of language, said with this horrible look on her face, as if she was eating lemons mixed with maggots.'

'Sounds like it was Latin,' said Nobby. 'A mate of mine went to a posh boardin' school an' they 'ad to learn Latin which is a nasty language which he says no one uses 'cept at posh schools. He reckoned it must be full of rotten magic 'cos the man who taught it was all shrivelled and wrinkled like he'd been shrunk in a washin' machine.'

'Just like Daz,' laughed Gwil. Old Whaley put 'em in one day and that's why he's so small.'

'I'd rather have a small body like Daz's than a small mind like yours,' said Rachel placidly, poking him in the side.

'When are we goin' to stop?' asked Nobby. 'We was up early and I need a rest.'

'*You* got up early!' said Rob indignantly. 'I never went to bed! After settin' the prisoners free, but before going to the palace at dawn, we were marchin' about in the night. First we ran into Ali, then we had a skirmish near the tunnels.'

'You haven't told us about that yet.'

'Sorry. I got confused about which part of the story I was on. We'd got back to the forest in the dark. Alice ran out and told us about the army gathered near the tunnels where most of the Muselings had been living. Dannos went off to investigate. He took a small group of creatures, and they must've run like a hurricane 'cos they were back before Ali and me had hardly finished catching up on what each of us had been doing. They said they needed us to come—as many as could be spared.'

'Do they live in tunnels, then?'

'They didn't till the Queen came. Only the black Muselings lived in the ground before that, but they all had to gang together once she started attacking their homes. Anyway, we marched to the hill where the tunnels start, and there was a lot going on already. The soldiers had discovered that no one was in (the other Muselings was all in the city, knocking holes in the factories). So the soldiers were busy setting up an ambush, and trying to catch Ballbody.'

'Catch who?'

'Ballbody's a friend of Alice. He's like a very large football, but heavy like he was made of stone. He kept rolling about like a cannonball, knocking them over and—most important of all—crashing into their carts. If he hadn't scuppered the carts, we'd have been lost.'

'I saw one of them, Robs—full of grenades, I thought.'

'That's almost it, Daz. They was gas grenades.' Robert stopped to cough again. 'They were makin' them in a factory. Old Ballbody knocked most of their supply into the bushes. Then we came up and ambushed the ambush. You should've seen the fight. There's this big woman Museling, black as Simey, wiv muscles like marrows. A soldier threw a grenade at her, and she caught it and then threw it so high in the air that it looked like it might hit the moon. She ran over to the Queen's right-hand man and lifted him from his saddle like he was a big teddy bear. He tried to cut her with his sword, but she whacked him one on the head and that was enough.'

They made approving noises.

'Was she the one that bent the Queen's sword?'

He nodded. 'Anyhow, the soldiers scattered and we spent the night moving the prisoners we'd set free into the tunnels. We also set up a hospital. A lot of creatures had got a dose of gas, or been cut by swords. Ballbody was covered with burns and bruises. But he was grinning all over and singing funny songs like it was carnival night. Alice looked after him.'

'Rob—what will happen to Alice?' Rachel looked at him seriously. 'Will they get there in time?'

'They go very fast....' His voice died away.

'How'd she get caught?'

'We was on the way back from the palace in the morning, flying our flag of truce, when one of those crow-things attacked us. We all scattered, 'cept Ali. She just stood there, calm as calm. As though she wasn't afraid at all. She had the flag, and when the thing flew at one of the Muselings, she walloped it over the head with the pole. It turned and would've snatched her up, but she stuffed the flag into its beak and knocked it onto its back.'

'You're makin' this up!' Nobby complained.

'Scout's honour, Nobby.'

'Yer ain't a Scout!'

'She was really wicked with that flag. I couldn't stop laughing, and I was too scared to move anyway. But just then, out of the woods come about twenty soldiers. We fought them, but more kept joining the battle. From both sides, too. Casca came out of the woods with a band of creatures—not Muselings, they was all sorts. Never saw such beasts. One of 'em had two heads! Soon we was swept back and when I next looked up, Ali was tied up and sittin' on a rock. I could tell by the look on her face that she wished she had that flag and pole in her hands again. That's when we were pushed back into the woods and they started throwing gas in after us.'

'Then?'

'The other Muselings came out of the woods. Then the cavalry came: you and Nobby and Daz and Gwil and Simey. You didn't 'alf give me a shock. I thought I was dead and dreaming.'

'You can't be dead *and* dreamin', Rob,' said Gwil.

'What I wonder is, where's the Rev?' asked Daz suddenly. He looked at Rachel, who shook her head. She had been brooding about two people for the last half-hour: Alice and Elias. When she was thinking, she usually didn't talk.

A detachment of Muselings had run ahead. They had no hope of cutting off the Queen's flight before she reached the palace; and they knew that they had little chance of doing anything once she was inside her own grounds. Her powers were greatest there. Not only would many soldiers have straggled back into the gates, but the Queen's spiritual stronghold was there too. Rachel was most uneasy. She knew now of the dread spell cast at the cave, where Alice was nearly buried alive. What were the limits of the Queen's power? She seemed able to blast people and things at will—sometimes. What was she now doing to Alice?

26

The House of Mirrors

Jess set Alice in a soft chair and removed her bonds. Alice ran immediately to the door, but it would not open. Jess walked, unhurried, to the table and poured two drinks from a long, cool-looking jug. She offered one cup to Alice, while drinking from the other. Alice would not look at her.

'You are very thirsty.'

That was true. Alice felt the force of thirst suddenly: a sweet throbbing in the throat and a longing in the stomach for soft, cool waters. From the cup came a fragrance of raspberries, promising luscious refreshment. She had to fight hard against her desire to accept.

The Queen, still in battle dress, walked to the other end of the room. They were high up in the house—in the attic, to judge from the narrow windows set in the slanted roof above them. The large square room was a cool mint-green colour. In its centre were two soft chairs by a low table, and in a corner was a folded screen.

The Queen began to extend this screen. At first it was simply a three-part expanse; but it grew as the Queen quietly unravelled it until it went about the room. Its panels glittered and shimmered; the liquid light from the high windows swirled round and round the mirrored surface, like water flying about a whirlpool. Looking at it made Alice giddy and uneasy.

The Queen sat in one chair. Despite herself, Alice walked to the other chair.

'I do think you could trust me, if only a little,' began the Queen. 'It would make all the difference if you would trust me. Together we might stop these senseless battles.' She paused, and repeated gently, 'You are very thirsty.'

That was doubly true now. And why should she not drink? They had eaten and drunk in the Queen's house before. Her hand nearly went to the cup. But stubbornness drove it back to her side. The fact that the Queen wanted her to drink was enough to keep her from doing so.

'You have come through many trials. You have done well. I thought you would. But it was necessary to prove you, for yourself.'

'What?' Alice's voice sounded thick and graceless to her own ears. By contrast, the Queen's voice had been pure and courteous.

'We all decided that you were the most likely to succeed. But the Muselings said that you must be proven first. I took their advice, as I have always done. When they come, in a few moments, they will be pleased that you have so excelled all our hopes.'

'You—and the Muselings—together? That's not true!'

'Yes, we played our parts well, did we not? I think Rachel and Robert were taken in, too. The Muselings were worried at first that you might guess we were only pretending to be enemies. It took all our concentration to see that there were no slips. When Mara comes, she will explain their side of the pretence. For my part, I merely had to act the part of the cruel Queen.' The Queen laughed.

'I don't believe you.'

'Then look!' The Queen pointed to the side. A door opened in the panels, and Eling, the old black Museling, stepped through. He bowed before the Queen, took her hand, and kissed it.

'Did she not do well, Your Highness?' he asked the Queen in his old, hoarse voice.

'Very well, Eling. She fought hard and deserves her reward.'

Eling bowed to Alice and took her hand. He smiled at her. She looked at him wonderingly. Then it was true.

'Come, drink, Princess! And do not doubt your friends!' he said. He was holding the cup now, and the wet smell made her thirstier than ever. She took the cool vessel in her left hand, as he held her right. She raised the cup to her lips.

His hand. What was it about the hand? It looked perfectly normal. The cup was so cool, and he held her hand in his cool, wrinkled old hand. His hand!

She threw the cup to the floor, and threw the hand from her.

As the cup crashed and shattered, the light went out. A snarling howl was cut short.

'Fool!' the Queen spat at the creature on the floor.

A hand, thought Alice: *but Muselings have paws. And they do not shake hands.*

Suddenly the light returned. The Queen was gone and Alice was alone. The door in the panel was open and unguarded. She flew to it and pushed through. A flight of steps led straight down to another door. She nearly fell down them. At the bottom she found the door unlocked. Suddenly suspicious, she pushed it open a crack and peered out. There was the side of the house; there, the wall which ran around it.

She could hear voices. Someone was rattling the gates at the front of the house. That was Robert's voice! And Rachel's! She rushed out, heedless. A tree grew by the wall, one which she had seen the other day. She noticed now, as she had not noticed then, that it would be just possible to climb it and from there get onto the wall. Almost crying with joy, she leapt at it. On the third attempt she was into its branches. She heard soldiers running from the house, but she was onto the wall and over.

Rob was there—he had seen her come over. He dragged her away from the wall.

'We'd better keep away from the house.'

'Rob! You're all right again! You looked so sick in the wood.'

'Yeah.' He coughed. Then he took a flask from his side and had a long draw at it. 'I'm much better now. We've come to make our peace with the Queen.'

'Peace?'

'There's been a lot of misunderstanding. She could be our friend, you know—and the Muselings' friend, too. We've got to give her a chance to prove herself. Want a drink?' He held the flask out to her.

'Yes. I'm dying of thirst.' She raised the flask. The soft smell of raspberries was wonderful. Then, puzzled, she lowered the flask again.

'Rob—I thought you didn't like raspberry.'

'I don't—that's strawberry. They smell almost the same.'

She sniffed it. It did smell more of strawberries, now that he had said that. But the smell of raspberries lingered too. And Robert's voice—he had spoken so clearly, without running his words together like he usually did. And he had said such odd things too.

She poured the flask onto the ground. Then she threw it against a tree. It broke into shining fragments. The tree broke too. When she turned, Robert was gone. She was alone outside the palace wall. Or was she?

She said loudly, 'I don't believe I'm outside the room I started in. And I'm not going to believe I'm outside it until I really am. And until I believe I'm outside, I'm going to sing songs. And I don't sing very well, I warn you.'

Her singing was not pleasant to listen to. She knew almost one hundred songs, but she didn't know the tunes very well. However, she could sing very loudly indeed, and she believed that this made up for the lack of tunefulness. She began now. After twenty minutes, when she was on her fifth song, the wall began to tremble before her eyes. During the sixth, the trees faded. Just as she started the seventh, the sky fell away with a whispered sigh, and she was once again sitting in the attic room. The Queen was in the other chair, her face covered with extreme annoyance. Her hands were over her ears, and her feet rested in a puddle of rose-coloured water which had spilled from the jug now in pieces upon the floor.

'He who would valiant be 'gainst all disaster,' Alice continued. This was one of her favourites. She generally preferred the modern songs they had in church, but this very old hymn had great charm. She began another verse of it.

'No hobgoblin or foul fiend shall daunt his spirit;
He knows he at the end shall life inherit.'

The Queen left, locking the door behind her.

Alice went immediately and folded up the mirror as best she could.

'I'd rather have the dreadfulest truth than have the wonderfulest lies,' she said to no one in particular. It was true. It was the one fact the Queen had not taken into account.

27

The Queen Fights Back

The Queen drew her chair up close to the desk and began to write in a small neat fashion on a lined pad of paper. She was summarising the situation.

First, the three children have not responded as I would have hoped. They have not recognised the true worth of tradition and of royal judgement. I have not been able to persuade them that it is to their own advantage for them to join forces with me. The possibility of privilege, position and wealth has not influenced them as it would a reasonable adult.

Second....

The summary went on for several minutes. When she had finished, she laid her pen on the table. Her brow wrinkled. She was thinking hard. She had not been able to interest Rachel at all. She had probably driven Robert far away from her. She had found Alice to be stubborn and simple.

It was unfortunate that she had lost her temper at the cave. Lrans had been furious and she had been weary. If she had destroyed the three of them when she had had them together, she could have preserved her rule for another century—or so the prophecies had suggested. If she had persuaded one to join with her, she could reign here for a thousand years...she had been a fool to try and win them all. But the reward had been so tempting—she could have re-entered Earth and set about conquering it again. But now...What should she do now?

Just as she decided her course, there was a knock on her study door. A guard came in when she called.

'Your Highness, the rebels have come to the gate.'

'I will come. Please fetch the girl from upstairs and bring her to me in the main hallway.'

She rose and went to the hall herself. The butler stood by the front door. She approached and signalled to him to open it. Fearless and proud, she swept through. At the gates, a band of Muselings and other creatures was gathered. She raised her voice and proclaimed: 'I will speak only to the two children!'

Then she returned to the hallway. Alice stood glaring defiantly at her. The Queen pretended not to notice.

'Better now, my dear? You were dreaming again, I fear. You were quite asleep when I brought you in from that nasty battle you got caught up with. When your brother and sister come, we'll have a lovely reunion, will we not?'

Alice wrinkled her nose at this attempt to talk away all that had happened. She said nothing.

The Queen nodded to a servant. 'Take her into the kitchen and find her something to eat and drink.'

Alice wrinkled her nose again. She wouldn't eat anything of the Queen's again, ever. A firm hand pulled her away.

As she went, the butler murmured something to the Queen, who then gestured that he should open the door a second time. The other humans had arrived. She swept outside again. 'The two of you may enter.' She nodded to Robert and Rachel.

Eling stepped forward to the gate and spoke. 'Do you expect the fly to return to the web it has just escaped?'

She laughed. 'Eling, your wisdom is wondrously seasoned with rich pictures like that one, and I congratulate you for it. But I mean no harm to these poor children. I alone can send them back home, and I alone can help their poor friend, Alice.'

'What's wrong with Alice?' asked Rachel.

'Come in and see.'

'No!' She and Robert spoke together, with violence.

'Then you will not discover what is wrong with her. But come, one of you at least must care enough about her to enter and see her? I know that boys are sometimes unkind towards girls, but surely a girl will have enough pity in her heart to come to the aid of another girl in an hour of need?' The Queen looked questioningly at Rachel.

'Why don't you bring her to us?'

'I would rather you trusted me. What wrong have I done you? And don't you care enough about Alice to brave my doors?'

Robert coughed and spoke hoarsely. 'You're not being fair. If coming into your house would help Ali, then of course we'd do it. But we don't do it to prove we trust you, 'cos we don't and that's all there is to it.'

'And you, Rachel? Do you agree with these harsh words? Your friend Robert seems quite willing to abandon Alice.'

'Well—' Rachel paused. The question muddled her. Surely Robert hadn't really said he would abandon Alice. Hadn't he said just now that he'd go if it would help?

'Come, Rachel,' persisted the Queen. 'The most important thing is to help Alice, isn't it? She attacked my soldiers and my creatures, but I have protected her from punishment and have doctored her as best I can. Will you not take on trust my concern for her, and come in?'

This was even more confusing. It was true that Ali had attacked the Queen's troops. But Robert had said this was because they had attacked first. *Robert* had said...It was odd, now that she thought of it, how many of her beliefs about the Queen were based on what Rob had told her. She hadn't heard Alice's side of the story, much less the Queen's. Rob alone had told her of the blasting at the cave, and of the attack by the soldiers on the tunnels.

And it was true that these Muselings were a warlike crew. Hadn't she seen them fight? Was it not just possible that there had been, all along, a terrible misunderstanding? Was it not fair that the Muselings should be expected to join in with the Queen's plan to raise the living standards of the country by building factories which could manufacture goods for sale? Maybe the Muselings had fought her all along, and she had only been defending herself.

The Queen watched Rachel coolly. She was waiting for the best moment for her next move. As Rachel opened her mouth to speak, the Queen turned to go, slowly and sadly.

'Wait!'

The Queen paused on the doorstep, her head tilted towards Rachel.

'Yes, little one?'

'I don't know about trusting you, but I'll come and see to Alice.'

The Queen shook her head sadly. 'You know that will not do, Rachel. You can hardly come into my house if you harbour ugly suspicions about me.'

Rachel looked to those at her side. Robert was scowling at her. Eling made no sign. Only Casca ventured to speak up.

'Speaks pretty, does Ruby Red-Lips here—'er words are the best part of 'er. I wouldn't give an acorn for anything she ever did, but she talks like a bird sings.'

Suddenly Rachel saw her choice. Odd how clear it was. Whatever the Queen might say, she had a choice between two groups of people—rather, of creatures. She looked about her. There was Rob, and the Muselings, and Nobby and the gang. On the other side were the Queen and Lrans and Ahab and more like them.

She took a deep breath. 'I *will* come in if it will help Alice. But if you talk about suspicions, yes, I have ugly suspicions about you. And I will continue to have them.'

The Queen went on smiling. She had played her last card but one. There was another left. And then—even then, she could not lose. She had the power to destroy everyone standing at the gate with a wave of her hand. Then she would continue her work of building up her forces until she was able to rid the land of the accursed creatures who opposed her.

She came close to the gate and spoke sternly.

'You appear to know nothing about the right—the God-given right, indeed—which rulers have to make laws, administer justice, and decide policy. I have an absolute right to deal with your 'friend' as I wish. The courts have already passed the sentence of death on her. You might have freed her from that fate by a small attempt at compromise. Now she will die.'

'No!'

'Oh, yes. And my terms are fair. I will sweep aside her sentence if you will return to your proper position as subjects in this land. Kiss my hand and swear obedience to the Royal Household, and she will join you in the next minute. Otherwise you will hear the sentence carried out with your own ears.' She pointed back to the palace.

They looked at her closely. She meant what she said. It would have been easier if they had come too late. Now they had to choose between doing something dishonest (swearing obedience) and something dishonourable (abandoning Alice). Which should they do?

As they tried to think, a noise of murmurings from behind them grew into cheers. They turned. What was it?

28

A Voice from the Past

A hand fell on each shoulder. Rachel looked up, and her face brightened.

'Elias!'

'The Rev!' Robert added, suddenly relieved. Elias would know the answer to the problem.

Elias was looking queerly at the Queen. She was looking at him just as oddly, as well she might. His face was smeared with smoke, and there were ashes in his hair and beard. His trousers were torn at the ankles, and beside him sat a small fox cub. He spoke first.

'I notice, Jezebel, that you have changed little. You still try to bully people with falsehoods. As if God had any more part in making you Queen than had my friend the fox here! If God had his way, you would be in your own dungeons, coming to repent of your evils.' As if to emphasise the old man's remarks, the fox yapped angrily through the bars of the gates at the Queen.

During this speech, the Queen had become pale as paste. When she spoke, her voice was high and tense: 'Elijah! I should have known there was something more to all this than three misbegotten children. I thought you dead, you false prophet; but that is soon remedied. Challenge my right to rule this land, will you? I will show you quickly enough who wields the power in this little world!'

She raised her hand and struck towards the gate. Robert flinched automatically, but he need not have bothered.

Nothing happened. Elias stood as before, leaning on his staff. A grim smile flickered across his wrinkled old face.

'I once ran from you, Jezebel. Then I was afraid of death. Now I am afraid no longer. Kill me, and I enter my reward; what have I to fear? But you—what awaits you? You have much to fear.'

She stared at him. Her lips were bright against her pale cheeks. As he spoke, her hands trembled.

'Come, Jezebel. I offer you one chance: turn now, and blot out the past. Release the girl. Restore this land to its beauty. And surrender to me. It is worth your while to do so, if only because of the fear I spoke of. And what else can you do? While I am here, you will have no great power; it has been taken from you. Even your bright flowers have been destroyed—every one.'

She looked left and right. Then she drew herself up, proud and determined. For reply, she spat on the ground, whirled about and ran into the house.

'Stop her!' Rachel cried. Alice was inside. There was murder in the haughty eyes which had despised Elias' offer.

Elias knocked at the gates with his staff, and they fell on the ground like so much aluminium foil. But as Rob and Rachel pushed through into the courtyard, they saw that they were too late.

Alice herself appeared at an open ground-floor window. With a clumsy lurch, she was over the sill and out on the ground. A small white-haired figure leapt over the sill after her and rolled over twice before springing up. It was Nancy.

They ran to the others: Alice to be wrapped in an embrace by Rachel, and Nancy to be slapped firmly on the back by Casca and Dannos.

'Easy boys! That shoulder hurts a mite. I'm not as young as I was.'

'Did you hurt yourself when you jumped out?' Rob wanted to know.

'Jumping out of a window? A little thing like that? I've jumped out of express trains in my time, shortie—a win-

dow's nothin'. Naw, I twisted it trying to hold one guard
down while whackin' another with a frying pan.'

A noise overhead cut short their congratulations. Two
black shapes were dropping quickly from the skies, straight
on the group at the gate. They scattered.

The crows attacked two separate groups. Ahab flew
straight at Elias and a small band of Muselings at the gate.
The other pursued the children across a small field, clawing
and snapping at them.

Rachel pulled Alice into the shade of one of three small
oak trees which stood perhaps fifty yards from the palace.
When she turned to look back towards the palace, she saw
that Nobby had come only halfway from the gates. He was
standing over one of the smaller boys, protecting him from
the crow-creature which hovered almost directly above his
head.

Nobby was slashing at the beast with a stout stick he had
found on the ground, and the crow was furiously trying to
beat past the stick so as to strike at his face. Unfortunately,
the stick was not quite sound: at each swing, part of it
would break off. As a result, with every swoop and dip, the
crow came a little closer. Nobby was forced steadily back,
and the boy on the ground (which turned out to be Simey)
crawled along with him, not daring to raise his head. Nobby
glanced behind him, appealing for help.

All at once Robert was there as well, swinging his own
stick and shouting to Simey to 'get out of the way!'. He and
Nobby fought with the creature blow for blow; and yet still
they were pressed back, and further back. Rachel glanced
beyond them, towards the gate, and saw that the group
fighting there was suffering a similar slow retreat.

Now all Nobby's fighting instincts were stretched to their
limit. He had found a better tree limb, and he danced in
with it, striking first at one part of the crow's body and then
another; then he would swerve aside, duck and move out of
reach of that angry beak and those clutching, fearful claws.
He kicked and spat and threw stones and dust at the
greedy, glittering eyes.

The others supported him as best they could. They broke their fingernails pulling stones from the ground, which they flung in the air as a steady hail, together with smaller sticks. Robert, already an experienced fighter in this war, rushed in with a flurry of blows whenever Nobby fell back with exhaustion or was caught by a sudden twisting dive of the crow.

Yet it was hopeless. Already they had picked up all the rocks within twenty yards. They had been pushed right up against the three trees. Nobby faltered more and more. He had changed hands several times already, and it was obvious that his strength was failing. Rachel swung into battle with her own stick, but also with a feeling of desperation. The creature seemed hardly to feel the blows rained on it; its beak was open in loud raucous cries of spiteful laughter as it swept down on them again and again. With a sickening jolt of realisation, Rachel knew that it had been playing with them all along, like a cat playing with a mouse. It could take one of them whenever it tired of its game.

Suddenly, it flung itself against one of the smaller boys, knocking Nobby and Rachel both aside as it did so. For a long moment it hovered about twenty feet overhead, its black eyes flicking from one child to the other, choosing which it should take first. Nobby threw himself into its path again, weakly raising his stick. The crow's eyes hardened on him. It folded its wings and dropped, intending to crush him with its weight.

Out of the corner of her eye, Rachel glimpsed a black blur. It was a shape which Alice had watched fearfully for the last few minutes as it galloped on all fours along the road, covering the last mile at a rate which was only just believable. It had been running for the last half hour, and had had no sleep for two nights, but in this last hundred yards its legs were a flashing black dynamo of speed which ended in a lunge through the air fully eight feet off the ground.

It crashed into the crow as that beast dropped onto Nobby, knocking it to one side and landing on it with a great crack of bones and tearing of flesh. A cloud of dust rushed into the air; the crow and its attacker rolled over several times, and then the crow lay still as the Black Museling rose shakily to her feet. It was Mara.

She stumbled over to the children, and then sat on the ground, her sides heaving as she gasped for breath. Seeing Alice, she held out her hand to her and Alice ran over and clasped it. The others crowded around her, tears of relief in their eyes. She smiled at them, but then she seemed to remember something, and she looked suddenly about.

She smiled grimly. 'And one to go,' she said, meaning the other crow. Rising, she set off at an unsteady run towards the gate, motioning to the children to remain where they were.

The children were relieved that they had no further part in the battle. They watched from beneath the trees as soldiers rushed from the gates (not nearly so many as they had seen in the woods earlier that day), and as the Queen herself emerged, swinging a sword. Her other crow fell to Mara; Elias was cut by a sword-thrust and sat watching from the gateway with his back to the wall as Eling himself fought the Queen to a standstill.

Although the old Museling was weaponless, and stood about half the Queen's height, he was hot with an anger which drove her back. He tore the Queen's weapons from her hands and wrestled with her on the steps of the palace. Finally, she fell back.

She looked about her. Her soldiers had nearly all surrendered. Her two crows lay lifeless, and no one came to her aid as she lay on the hard steps at her own door. It was the end. She smiled bitterly. But she would have her revenge. There were spells she knew—terrible spells against which there was little defence. She had spent long years learning them and gaining the power to say them. She would utter them. She began to mumble them to herself as she watched her chance to flee. Suddenly she darted to her doors, flinging Casca down the steps as if he were a doll. She slammed the doors behind her and bolted them. Now!

Elias stood in the hallway before her, leaning on his walking stick and holding his left side. 'Jezebel, do you not know the final law?'

She looked at him dully. She continued to mutter the spell under her breath. She was halfway through it. She shook her head.

'The final law states that all you do comes back upon yourself. Think! All you do and say! In life it is not so. But in the end...in the end, all comes back upon you.'

She nodded. She did not care. She would destroy them all, or at least so spoil their lives and their worlds that they would beg for destruction. Just a few phrases more, and she would have finished.

'Stop! Don't you see it is no good? You will destroy yourself!'

She had finished now. She wiped her face on her sleeve and drew herself up stiffly, staring into his eyes. She said, meaning each word, 'I don't care what I do.'

Then the change came. The world rocked and squealed like a wild, crazy animal. Outside, everyone was thrown to the ground. The palace began to crumble.

29

Part of the End

Rachel and the other children watched, unable to blink, as the palace shivered. Then with a shrieking roar it collapsed on itself, crushing all within it. A great cry, as of some grotesque demon, burst through the cascading stone and timber. Then there was silence for a few seconds. After this there came to their ears the sounds of destruction elsewhere in the city the Queen had created. Houses and factories dissolved into rubble, like sugar cubes collapsing when water is poured on them.

People and creatures began to stand up shakily, but were immediately thrown to the ground again by a rumbling explosion. The remains of the castle boiled and then burst into flame. A smell of sulphur and hot metal hit them, followed by a sudden wave of intense heat.

Everyone who was near the palace and could still move began to walk or crawl away. Others who lay on the ground were dragged away by those nearby. In a few minutes' time, the heat was so powerful that the children standing nearly one hundred paces away had to move further back. Angry, crackling flames rushed into the sky, pushing an acrid black smoke before them. The very bricks of the destroyed building cracked and crumbled in the heat; glass from the shattered windows melted and ran on the scorched earth like water spilt on a blackened carpet.

Rachel was crying. They had seen Elias go inside, and he had not returned. The fox nosed her hand, whimpering. It settled onto its chest with its head on its paws and its eyes fixed on the searing blaze, waiting for its master to come out. Rachel knelt and stroked its fur. After half an hour, the fire had not diminished; but still they sat together in hopeless hope. About them creatures came and went, removing the wounded and dead. Alice sat a few yards off with Nobby and Rob and the others, telling of her own adventures.

Finally, they returned to the tunnels. There was much shouting and rejoicing at first, but it soon died away. Everyone was simply too tired to celebrate. Rachel, Robert, Alice and the others from the Home climbed stiffly onto soft beds and collapsed into a heavy sleep.

Not for several days did they recover their spirits. The emotions of battle and its results had drained everyone. Even Casca was subdued. War was terrible, even when good triumphed. The killing or maiming of living creatures, and the dreadful arguments and horrid feelings were even more unpleasant to remember than they had been to see. For a few days they discussed their recent battles with reluctance, and the Muselings treated their former enemies with undeserved kindness. It would have puzzled the Queen to have heard how she was spoken of by the creatures who had fought her, for they referred to her with respect and spoke of her death with evident regret.

Casca commented once: 'A woman like that—turned right way round—why, she'd waken life in a dead stone. She'd make the sun shine brighter, she would. More's the shame she lived 'er life inside out and backwards.'

What finally changed the atmosphere was the day when the dead were buried. Many creatures and people were set to rest in a broad meadow, in a quiet and solemn time of remembrance. But as the last prayer was said, the group of creatures suddenly began to sing, at first so softly that you noticed the music no more than you would notice the mildest of breezes on a summer's day. Then the sound swelled until the words and notes swept around the meadow like a gale. Yet it was not loud and oppressive; it filled the air not by sheer volume but by the fullness of the music and the beauty of the words—words often strange to the children, but vibrating with hidden meaning.

The music seemed to penetrate each cell of their bodies and send them tingling. It made them want to cry, and then to dance and clap. A sense of wonder—of solemn awe and fearful joy—swept through them, and they were floating in a sea of joy which flowed on and on to the end of the worlds.

When the singing finished, they found that they had walked, almost in a dream, back to the caves for dinner. Here there was sudden and real rejoicing. Light had come on them, and they remembered all things without the dragging sadness they had known.

They spoke at length of those they had known but who had now gone. The smallest squirrel which had perished in battle was spoken of for almost an hour. His earlier words were recalled; his deeds; and most of all, his jokes and pranks.

This recalling continued in small groups for many days, and it seemed to wash away any heaviness remaining in their hearts. The stories about the fallen were often comical, and laughter rang in the Muselings' meeting places. The days of mourning had run their course, and the days of feasting began. In the tunnels and in encampments which the Muselings set up in the nearby woods, merry games were played, and riotous songs were sung.

It was obvious that the Muselings held in their minds a wealth of stories about their world. They could remember in detail conversations held a hundred years before. They could remind one another of small actions done by their great-grandparents. Nobby and Simey and Daz and Gwil, who had taken to Mara as their champion, sat for hours, open-mouthed, as she told of battles fought over several centuries and recounted humorous stories of long ago.

'Crumbs!' breathed Daz at one point. 'You oughter write that down an' put it in a book!'

'What is that?' asked Mara, puzzled.

'Y'know, write it out.'

'But why? I shall always remember it, and I can retell it whenever anyone is pleased to hear of it again.'

'But Tiny,' Nobby put in, 'surely you've got books of stories an' such—an' school books for learning out of?'

She laughed and shook her head. 'I know the Queen (God rest her soul) had many such "books". But we have not such things. Perhaps it is good to have books. And yet, when you write your thoughts onto a page, is something lost from them? Sometimes it must be better to tell the thoughts living from your lips.'

'And no school books neither?'

Mara shook her head solemnly.

'Smashin'!' exclaimed Daz.

'Can we stay 'ere, then?' Gwil and Simey choroused.

'Whaley can't chase us out of bed 'ere and make us do our maths before breakfast,' Nobby added.

But it was not to be. They knew already that they would be returning. All they were waiting for was news of when that would be. Eling had told Rachel that he would be able to guide them back to where they had entered his land— 'when the time comes'. Meanwhile they were to enjoy their holiday.

Of course, there were not only the children to consider. Several thousand humans remained, who had been soldiers or factory workers. Eling had called them together and offered a choice: they might return to the other world, or else stay and live out their time among his creatures.

'But you must understand,' he warned them, 'that you will be visitors in our land, and you will have to obey our laws. There will be no business, no shops, no eating of meat. You may build houses, and we will help you. You may grow food, and we will teach you how this is done. But there will be no machines and no money. What each person or creature has will be shared with his fellows. Moreover, you must understand that this is a slow land. We do not rush from one day to the next. We work hard, and then we pause for refreshment. Ours is a land of peace, of song, of praise for what we have received. We do not spend our days worrying about tomorrow; we spend them enjoying today.

'And there will be no children. Other creatures and Muselings will once again have young; but no human children will there be. Yours will be the last generation of your people to live here.'

It is perhaps surprising that all the Queen's people but two decided to stay under these conditions. The two who wished to leave were Nancy and Lrans. Lord Lrans had already gone: he had escaped from the tunnels where he had been held prisoner, and had been chased to the same hole the children had last entered the country by. The Muselings had not followed him.

Nancy's decision was explained by her like this: 'I've always wanted to see England. Sure enough, if I could pick a place to live, I think I'd live here and play out my days makin' cookies an' playin' with baby Muselings. But I ain't seen England yet, and I reckon this is my last chance.'

She gave Casca and Dannos a hug each; they looked distraught to lose her. 'We've had some good times together, boys. Now, don't fuss. It's not over yet, not by a long throw. There's life in the old girl yet, and maybe you'll see me again this side of the other place.'

'*I'm* glad you're coming,' said Robert. 'You were going to teach me some wrestling holds.'

'Yer,' agreed Nobby. 'And you was goin' to show us how to whistle using your fingers, an' lots of other things too.'

Casca wiped his eyes and chuckled. 'Leastways, Nancy, we now know you'll be properly employed teachin' good manners and deportment to these poor humans. Wonder-Rob here, he needs a bit o' training up. We'll miss you, though...like losin' an arm, this is.'

'I wish we didn't have to go.' This was from Alice. She held Rachel's hand. After a week spent with these creatures, she felt this place to be home as much as anywhere else. 'I'm even learning how to sing properly.'

The others laughed. This little world had now absorbed Alice's fund of songs, and you could not walk far without hearing a stirring chorus sung by a group of Muselings, improvising and improving the tunes no end. Then, strangely, there would be another group singing 'Baa Baa Black Sheep' in a land where there were no sheep.

Rachel, however, was ready to leave. Followed each time by the little fox, she had wandered daily through the woods, always to end up near the ruin which had been the palace. She found it more difficult than the others to laugh and join the celebrations. Yes, this was a good place. Yes, she liked and was fast coming to love the creatures. But a sadness had settled on her heart, together with a yearning for she knew not what. When she tried to explain it to the others, the words would not come together into the shape of her thoughts. She gave up trying to understand it herself.

The Muselings seemed to know how she felt. Mara would lay a giant paw gently on her shoulder for a minute, kiss her on the top of the head, and gaze with her into the sky for an hour at a time. No words were exchanged, merely a gentle understanding. She had finished her task here; something else called her back into her own world.

It helped to talk of Elias. She was surprised to discover that the Muselings had known of him already. On the last day, she found Eling in a talkative mood.

'The old one. He has been before—not in this world, but in others. Even the Queen knew of him. He was in the book she called *The Words*. They called him simply the Prophet then. I do not think he was popular with her.' Eling waved his hand as he spoke. 'He has been in many worlds. It was said he would come to ours. A small heaven is this, nearer to the centre than the others; yet we had hoped he would come. We hoped also that he would stay. Now he is lost.'

Rachel told him some of what she knew. 'He said he had run from her before. She was a Queen in our own world. She threatened him, and he fled to the mountains. That is written in our Bible. I remember him reading out his own story once—but his name was different then. They called him Elijah.'

Time now passed so quickly; the children were left with

jumbled memories of war and peace, of talking, singing, trying new food, and listening: to Ballbody, who knew more poems and stories of more worlds than they would ever have time to hear; to Casca, who wanted to tell them of his mother who had once fallen into an underground lake but swam until she reached the place where it emptied into the stream; to Mara, who told them of the bravery of the Tove which had fallen in the last battle at the gates.... And suddenly they had come to the last meal of their last day.

Feather had produced soft sweet rolls in which a swirl of brown sugar followed a trail of small nuts from the outside to the centre. They sipped their last cup of 'cocoa' and then went to bid final goodbyes to their friends. There were warm furry hugs, and many tears. And then, the hardest moment of all—the moment of setting out with Dannos and Casca for the hole between the worlds.

30

The End of the Beginning

They ran across the road by the church. Robert still saw in his mind the final quizzical smile of Dannos as he had held out his paw to be slapped. 'Go it, boy wonder!' he had cried. And Casca had added, 'If the Elizabeth Mayhem Orphanage can take two more, an' your boss-lady don't mind 'em furry, let us know, Wobbit!'

Here, the sun shone. They realised that they had been expecting rain. Past the church, a car was turning into Bridge Street. Nancy looked at it with interest.

'Models have moved on a bit since I was around,' she commented.

Rachel glanced into the church porch. The fox cub had insisted on coming with them, and he had scooted up into the church as soon as they had crossed the road. Now he was sadly coming out again. They stopped to read the church notice-board, which had a large white label pasted onto it, covering the place which would normally give the telephone number of the Rector. Another number had been substituted. Rachel stared at it blankly and turned numbly to continue up the road.

'Back to the 'Ole,' muttered Nobby. Then he grinned. 'No more bread an' nuts every meal—bacon an' eggs again! Sausages!'

'Fish fingers!' added Gwil.

'Beefburgers and chips!' said Daz.

They were all smiling now except for Rachel. They came

to the rectory garden, and would have passed by so as to climb the hill to the Home. However, they had to turn into the garden because Mrs Welter came from the rectory and commanded them to 'Come here this very moment, or I'll....'

She shook her large arm at them in a meaningful manner, and they walked sheepishly to her at the rectory door.

'What on earth have you children been up to? Here I am trying to explain to the police that Mr Welter hasn't cut you up and fed you to the ducks, and trying to set things straight at the rectory after the fire, and you come waltzing out of the woods like you had been on a pleasant stroll there this last fortnight.'

'We ain't been up to nothin' on earth, Mrs W.'

'Simon, don't you give me any cheek. If it weren't that guests were coming to the Home this afternoon, I'd hang you all by your ears in a corner. Which would improve your appearances rather than otherwise.' She scowled at them, and they grinned back. They knew from her voice that they were forgiven. 'Now, you all just come inside and give me a hand moving things. If you show a bit of effort, I might just give you lunch later. Else you can go back to Flashetts and chew watercress.'

They entered, once she had swung her ponderous weight through the door. The kitchen was a blackened mess. Obviously, there had been a fire within. Rachel shuddered as she looked at it. She was too much reminded of another fire, more than a week ago.

Mrs Welter was muttering to herself. 'Men! Can't boil an egg without the fire brigade having to stand by!' Then she noticed Nancy standing in the doorway, next to a fox.

'What the blazes? Who are you, madam? Don't bring that creature in here!'

Another voice spoke from the passage to her right. 'That's all right, Mrs Welter. I expect that is my new housekeeper. I've been expecting her for some days now. I thought she might bring a pet with her.' Elias limped through into the kitchen.

'Elias!' shouted half a dozen voices at once.

Then a far louder voice resumed control. 'Rector!' scolded Mrs Welter. 'You get straight back into your bed. Tomorrow the Doctor said, tomorrow you can wander about as you please. But till then you're to rest. Those burns have hardly healed even now, and you'll put your leg out again.'

The children looked at him in delight. He was bandaged down one side, and had a leg in plaster about the ankle, but he was very much alive. His eyes twinkled as he looked them over.

'Well, well!' he exclaimed. 'I've been waiting for you these ten days! Surely it's not taken you all that time to find your way out!'

Mrs Welter waved him back into the passage.

'You go lie down,' she ordered, 'and I'll send Rachel in with a cup of tea for you. Then you can tell her about the fire. You're forgetting that they won't know anything about what's happened here.'

He smiled broadly. 'Oh, I don't know, Mrs Welter. I think they have a better idea than most about what has happened.' He kissed Rachel, Alice and Nancy, shook hands with the boys and stroked the fox cub.

'Perhaps you could show my housekeeper where the tea things are, Mrs Welter—and explain to her about the making of it. She's not a native of this country.... And if you can spare these reprobates for a few hours, I'm giving a little party tomorrow to which they are invited. And I have some work for them to do.' He smiled at them again. They all smiled back, including Rachel. He had a gleam in his eye which implied not only that this was a happy ending, but perhaps also a happy beginning.

Elijah, Ahab and Jezebel

Thousands of years ago someone named Ahab became King of Israel. He was a man who found it hard to make up his mind. He started by believing in God, but then decided to worship something called Baal instead. It was partly his wife Jezebel who talked him into this; she had grown up believing in Baal. She was a tough woman, for although Ahab ruled Israel, Jezebel ruled Ahab.

In Israel there lived a good man, a great prophet named Elijah. God sent him to tell Ahab to change his ways, but Ahab took no notice. Then Elijah told Ahab and Jezebel to call together all of Baal's top men. In a showdown on top of a mountain, Elijah showed that God was real and that Baal was a fake.

This was not the end of the story of Elijah, and you can read the rest in the Bible in the *First Book of Kings*, starting at chapter 17, and in the first two chapters of the *Second Book of Kings*.